The Kids Under the Stairs

Ben Y
and the Ghost in the Machine

K.A. Holt

chronicle books·san francisco

A very special thanks to Em Brewington and Alejandra Oliva,
whose insightful, educational, and thoughtful readings were
intrinsic to the creation of this book.

Library of Congress Cataloging-in-Publication Data available.

ISBN 978-1-4521-8321-3

Manufactured in China.

Design by Jennifer Tolo Pierce.
Typeset in Fedra Mono, Cultura New, Air, GFY Ralston,
FG Alex, FG Joe, and Karmatic Arcade.
Illustrations by K.A. Holt.
Hand-lettering by Isaac Roy.

10 9 8 7 6 5 4 3 2 1

Chronicle Books LLC
680 Second Street
San Francisco, California 94107

Chronicle Books—we see things differently. Become part
of our community at www.chroniclekids.com.

This book is dedicated to *you*.

I see you.
I'm proud of you.
I love you.

BEFORE

SB10BEN: heyyyyyy! you found it!

0BenwhY: sign in the public n00b beta server, pop a fairy, fly to the 2nd rainforest
0BenwhY: go 2 teleporter in the tree that looks like Mom's hair when it's raining—
0BenwhY: that's an epic journey to meet u at an abandoned n00b cabin, bro

SB10BEN: Remember the code I gave you? Type it in on the little sign right here.

0BenwhY: did i do it right?
0BenwhY: whoaaaa. 😲 what IS this place?

SB10BEN: My secret in-game lab!
SB10BEN: so I can test out new potions and tools and experimental stuff
SB10BEN: Technically not allowed at work, but I hate the sterile Q&A environment

OBenwhY: blerg blahb grown-up talk

OBenwhY: ooooh! what's this? A skylight TO SPACE?

OBenwhY: is that flying fire? ahh! watch out!

OBenwhY: is that chicken inside out? Gross!

SB10BEN: See? that's why I built this place! Invent, mess up, test stuff my bosses might not like

SB10BEN: And maybe 😈 one day I can leak things to the public to prove it's still *my* company (and to prove my bosses wrong)

OBenwhY: Benicio! 😨 why would u do that? Won't u get fired?

SB10BEN: Not if it stays a secret 😉

OBenwhY: but I thought u said nothing online can ever stay a secret

SB10BEN: what! you *listened* to something I said! 😨
SB10BEN: it's true, you have to always believe that anything you put online could be seen by anyone
SB10BEN: but this is a little different.

OBenwhY: how?

SB10BEN: no one is looking for it. and if no one is looking for it, no one can find it.

OBenwhY: 😕

SB10BEN: Just trust me, okay.
SB10BEN: No one is getting in trouble.

OBenwhY: and no one can get fired?

SB10BEN: Don't worry about any of that.
SB10BEN: Just worry about all the zillions of cool new ideas and inventions we're about to, uh . . .

OBenwhY: think of and invent?
OBenwhY: and did you just say WE????????

SB10BEN: Ha. Yes!
SB10BEN: You don't think like everyone else, kiddo. You have a unique brain.
SB10BEN: I'd love your help. Will you help me?

OBenwhY: ooooh what's this squishy thing?

SB10BEN: not sure yet. it might end up being building material that can float. 🤔

0BenwhY: you should call it starstone!

SB10BEN: love it. See? That's why I need your help.

0BenwhY: It'll just be you and me? Inventing secret stuff? Hanging out in chat? No one else?

SB10BEN: Just you and me. Inventing secret stuff. Hanging out in chat. No one else.

ΘBenwhY: I know you're not here

ΘBenwhY: I know the blocks won't build themselves

ΘBenwhY: I know the cool potions won't invent themselves

ΘBenwhY: I know you're not coming back

ΘBenwhY: but you said you'd be back

ΘBenwhY: and you ALWAYS do what you say

ΘBenwhY: so maybe you will come back

ΘBenwhY: even though I know it's impossible

ΘBenwhY: . . .

ΘBenwhY: but . . . we MADE the impossible, remember? Right here!

ΘBenwhY: You always said that. Sandbox makes the impossible possible.

ΘBenwhY: And since you always do what you say, I think the transitive property means—

ΘBenwhY: Boom, you could show up any second.

ΘBenwhY: that's just easy math.

ΘBenwhY: . . .

ΘBenwhY: . . .

ΘBenwhY: you know what's not easy?

0BenwhY: when i log into our chat, even though i know better
0BenwhY: and when I read the archive you kept *so we never lose any good ideas*
0BenwhY: when I just watch the cursor blink
0BenwhY: hoping one day
0BenwhY: you'll appear
0BenwhY: you'll say this has all been a very very very long bad dream
0BenwhY: . . .
0BenwhY: I should stop doing this. That's what you should *really* say.
0BenwhY: get a life, Benny.
0BenwhY: stop torturing yourself, Benny.
0BenwhY: go outside and get some fresh air, Benny.
0BenwhY: but you can't say that
0BenwhY: ghosts can't talk

WHO

HOME

Everything was great
until it wasn't.

It was all planned out
until it wasn't.

I had control
until I didn't.

I had HAIR
until I didn't.

▫ ▫ ▫ ▫

Esme,
a living bird chirp,
a goof made of snorts,
a tiny human,
an annoying hiccup
burping in my face
every day
all the time,
Esme,
my little sister,
says:

Don't worry.
People love scarecrows.

Slowly,
gently,
she reaches out,
like she would
to pet a newborn kitten
or a scared puppy.

It's so weird and gross.
I just want to touch it.

Esme,
a living bird chirp,
a goof made of snorts,
a tiny human,
my little sister,
is about to get smacked.

◦ ◦ ◦ ◦

It's cool and weird that you think people love scarecrows,
Esme, even though I think you are probably definitely wrong
about that. I also think maybe for your own safety you should
only say words like weird *or* gross *in your own head and not*
out loud because Ben Y will definitely yank your arm right off

*if you get any closer to her and she's a LOT taller than I am
so I'm not much help protecting you which I probably wouldn't
try to do anyway because my loyalty is with your sister. Sorry.*

I glare at Jordan.

*NOT sorry, I mean. I am not sorry to not protect you if your
sister tries to beat you up with the arm she just yanked off your
body.*

I lunge toward Esme,
but stop
when I feel a flutter,
like a falling whisper
float past
my cheek.

*I'm sensing a lot of feelings right now and that's fine and okay
because we all have big feelings when big things happen, and—*

Jordan,
who is MY friend
(not Esme's)
and who has
(very recently)
had a couple of sessions
with Mo,
who is a therapist

(and not an extra mom or a teacher)
seems to
(all of a sudden)
know a LOT
about feelings
and how to feel them.

Maybe Esme should stand over here out of smacking reach
and maybe Ben Y, you should stay where you are by the sink
because your hair doesn't seem to be finished disintegrating
and it should probably do that over the sink unless you want
to move to the bathtub for easier cleanup? Esme, NO, get over
here by me. Just touch all the hair on the floor. There's more
of it than on Ben Y's head anyway—

Jordan is NOT
the boss of me.
No one is the boss of me.
No one ever has been.
No one ever will be.

But Jordan IS my friend,
and I haven't had a lot of friends,
so he gets a special pass,
which means his words
are allowed into my brain
and not immediately shut out,
like most words

I don't want to hear
from most people
I don't want to listen to.

◻ ◻ ◻ ◻

Mistake number one:
putting Esme in charge
of the timer.

No. Wait.

Mistake number one:
putting Jordan in charge
of the bleach.

No. Wait.

Mistake number one:
putting myself in charge
of thinking
anything
could be done
to make me
seem interesting
to anyone.

◻ ◻ ◻ ◻

It's just that—
and this is the
actual,
for real
truth . . .

I've never,
not one time,
ever
met a kid
or seen a kid
as cool
as Ace,
the new kid,
with the who-cares
cosplay look,
with a different wig
every day,
pink
or
blue
or
any color
of the rainbow.

And when weasel-nosed
Vice Principal
Mr. Mann
yells, Ace!
DRESS CODE!
Take that thing off!
Ace takes that thing off
and underneath
has hair
the exact same color,
hahaha,
like a magic trick,
like a big ol' fart noise
right in the direction
of Mr. Mann's
sniffing
weasel nose,
and I just . . .
I don't even dare
to want to be that cool,
I just want to be
on the same planet
as cool like that.

□ □ □ □

And all of THAT
is why it seemed smart
to light a flare
and send it into the sky,
a message that said,
Hey! Ace! Notice me!

So I thought I might try
my own cosplay approach,
I might color my own hair
in some bright color
or even a whole rainbow
surrounding my face
and Ace would finally see me
and be like,
Wow, who are you supposed to be?
And I would say,
Oh, no one you've ever heard of,
and we'd both laugh and laugh,
and then I didn't think past that,
even though I was thinking
A LOT
about how our conversation might go
while the bleach dissolved,
while the shiny black
was sacrificed

to be reborn
as a rainbow.
And I got lost in my thoughts
and Esme pushed OFF
on the timer without telling anyone
and Jordan was busy figuring out
if he could fit the whole rainbow
on my head
or if one or two colors
might pack more punch,
and so all that was going on
when I was like,

Ow.

And Jordan was like,

Huh?

And I was like,

Ow ow ow OW,
get it off, get it off!

And Jordan was like,

Is it time already?

And Esme was like,

Oh, was that *what the timer was for?*

And Jordan was like,

WHAT.

And I was like,

MY HEAD IS ABOUT TO MELT GET OUT OF THE WAY.

And as I bowed my head
into the sink . . .
And as I prayed for my head
to stay unmelted . . .
And as I rinsed the bleach
out of my hair . . .
I wondered if maybe
there was a less painful way
to get Ace to notice me.

◻ ◻ ◻ ◻

But, yeah.
Too late for THAT idea.

◻ ◻ ◻ ◻

Half an hour later,
when my hair was dry
and splintering off
in straw-colored clumps,
covering the bathroom floor
like a hayloft,
I realized there would be no way
for Ace
to NOT notice me now.
There would be no way
for anyone
to STOP noticing me now,
because it was becoming
very apparent
very quickly
that my cosplay plan
had dissolved
just like my hair.

□ □ □ □

What if you shave the rest of your head to even things out,
and then when anyone asks, just say you had a super-great
cosplay idea and that you decided to fully commit to being
Avatar: The Last Hairbender?

Dang it!
Jordan always makes me laugh
even when I'd rather be crying.

We laugh and laugh
and laugh and laugh
and Jordan gets out the clippers,
the ones I haven't seen
since Benicio lived here,
and he smooths out my head,
and then rubs it for luck,
and that's when I stop laughing
and start crying
and confess to him
I might not be able to stop.

This may or may not be the best time to tell you this,

my best friend
talking jackhammer
saving grace
warm light of Never Quiet
says,

because you seem pretty mindfragile right now, which is
totally fine and understandable—

I make a note
to add
mindfragile
to the list I'm keeping
of Jordan's made-up,
but super-smart
words.

—but I think your mom is home.

▫ ▫ ▫ ▫

Oh, mija.
I am too tired to deal with this.

That's what Mom said
after her eyes
almost popped right out
of her head
but then just as quickly
closed tight,
shutting out the sight
of my bald head
and the giant mess.

A big splattering sneeze
loud enough
for the whole neighborhood
and maybe the whole planet
to hear,
exploded
from behind
the shower curtain.

Hello, Jordan,
Mom said,
eyes still closed.

Hi, Ms. Ybarra,
Jordan said,
still behind
the shower curtain,
as if it could
somehow
still hide him.

Mom's eyes opened,
but quickly closed again
as she shook her head
and walked out
toward the kitchen.

Clean it up, mija,
she yelled as she walked.
Then, a pause:
Do you need a ride home, Jordan?

No, ma'am.
Jordan's shout echoed
from the bathtub,
hollow.

Jordan stepped out of the tub,
faced me,
and said,
Yep. I was right. Your mom is home.

I slugged him,
soft,
in the shoulder,
and we laughed
stifled, snorting, giggles
as we shut the door,
and he called his mom
to come get him,
fast.

□ □ □ □

We cleaned up.
Jordan went home.
Everything seemed quiet.
So.

I tiptoed
into the kitchen,
and here I am,
fixing myself dinner,
a bowl of the finest
knock-off cereal
anyone could wish for.

Did you at least do your homework?

Mom appears silently,
like a ghost,
but not like the ghost
I'd like to see.

She leans her head back,
stares at the ceiling,
doesn't move,
like she's superglued
to the kitchen wall.

Some of it.
My answer dribbles cereal
back into the bowl.

Also, my answer is
maybe not the truth.

Esme leans her head around,
almost upside down,
peering through
the kitchen doorway.

No one asked me,
but guess what:
I really do like your hair, Benny.
Or, I guess, I like your head.
Don't be sad about it.
Once it gets fuzzier,
and once the black comes back,
you'll look so much like Benicio.
Even more than before.
My heart will like that.

Mom's head snaps up,
away from the wall,
as she smooths her hands
down the front of her scrubs,

as her voice sighs out:
It's late. Time for prayers, Esme.
Then bed.

And that is that.

Mom herds Esme off to her room,
for the nighttime prayers
they continue to whisper
day after day,
and that I continue to refuse
day after day,
and I am left at the table.
Still eating my soggy cereal.
Still bald.
Still me.
Still alone.
Day after day.

NOW

OBenwhY: I said I would never come back.

OBenwhY: To your room.

OBenwhY: Yeah, it's still YOUR room.

OBenwhY: You didn't have to win that argument quite so dramatically, you know.

OBenwhY: Anyway.

OBenwhY: I haven't been here since . . .

OBenwhY: since forever.

OBenwhY: But here I am

OBenwhY: . . .

OBenwhY: . . .

OBenwhY: Why are you in my room, grasshopper?

OBenwhY: That's what you'd say.

OBenwhY: if you were chatting with me instead of . . . me chatting with me

OBenwhY: I'd say, well, funny story . . .

OBenwhY: and you'd do a clapping emoji and a popcorn emoji

OBenwhY: . . .

OBenwhY: only it isn't a funny story.

OBenwhY: not really

OBenwhY: you'd say: not *yet*, grasshopper. It isn't a funny story *yet*

OBenwhY: and then you'd let me blow something up with an experimental potion

OBenwhY: . . .

OBenwhY: So.

OBenwhY: I shaved my head.

OBenwhY: and your room looks exactly the same as it did when you left

OBenwhY: and I just blew up a goat

OBenwhY: in Sandbox. Not in your room.

OBenwhY: I thought you might like to know.

OBenwhY: that's my not-funny story

BEFORE

SB10BEN: Grasshopper! You're here! Finally!

SB10BEN: I have a great plan for us today.

0BenwhY: Benicio!

0BenwhY: Look at this mess. 😬

0BenwhY: Stop turning chickens inside out!

0BenwhY: Didn't you see the change I made to that feather potion recipe?

SB10BEN: Not yet. I've been busy pondering something else.

SB10BEN: What if I teach you a superpower today?

0BenwhY: like how to pretend you're doing hard grown-up work when you're actually playing Sandbox with your little sister? 😊

SB10BEN: har har. I AM working. I get paid to play, remember? 😎

0BenwhY: what superpower are you talking about?

0BenwhY: I already know how to fly.

0BenwhY: you just pop a fairy over your head and use the dust to zoom around. easy.

SB10BEN: Not in the game.

SB10BEN: IRL

OBenwhY: U CAN TEACH ME 2 FLY IRL

SB10BEN: No, silly. something better.

SB10BEN: A gift to you before you go to middle school.

OBenwhY: will it help me pass the stupid FART?

OBenwhY: that really WOULD be a superpower

SB10BEN: omg, that Rigorous Assessment garbage is still a thing?

SB10BEN: Trust me. This is something actually useful.

SB10BEN: For middle school and beyond.

OBenwhY: WELL, TELL ME ALREADY. OR TEACH ME. OR WHATEVER.

SB10BEN: So impatient, my little grasshopper.

SB10BEN: okay, okay.

SB10BEN: Would you . . .

SB10BEN: like the ability . . .

SB10BEN: to become . . .

SB10BEN: . . . invisible?

SB10BEN: 👻 👻 👻

SB10BEN: Any time you want?

OBenwhY: wut

OBenwhY: u can't be serious.

SB1OBEN: Go look on the front porch. IRL.

SB1OBEN: There should be a small package addressed to you.

OBenwhY: !!!!!

OBenwhY: brb

OBenwhY: Got it! U got me a present?? Can I open it???

OBenwhY: It's not even my birthday or anything.

SB1OBEN: You're about to be a middle schooler, grasshopper!

SB1OBEN: That's big.

SB1OBEN: Yeah . . . open it.

OBenwhY: Uh. Hot-pink earbuds?

OBenwhY: Isn't hot pink the opposite of invisible?

SB1OBEN: Ah, but it's not.

SB1OBEN: When you're in the halls, or at lunch, or
wherever, pop those babies in and pretend to be jamming

OBenwhY: jamming? 😄

SB1OBEN: shut up

OBenwhY: 🤓

SB10BEN: let your eyes glaze over, like you're lost in your favorite song.

SB10BEN: don't look directly at anybody.

SB10BEN: No one will know you're listening to them

SB10BEN: Trust me. When people see you bopping in those earbuds . . .

0BenwhY: bopping?? 😄 😎 😎 😎

SB10BEN: you'll be invisible to them.

SB10BEN: Believe it.

SB10BEN: you'll be right there, but invisible. And you'll hear everything.

0BenwhY: why do i want to hear everything?

SB10BEN: why wouldn't you? you'll hear gossip. Secrets. You'll be the first to know big news.

SB10BEN: people will even talk about YOU while you're standing right there. If they think you can't hear.

0BenwhY: Why do I want to hear people talk about me behind OR in front of my back?

SB10BEN: so you know who your real friends are, grasshopper. Trust me.

SB10BEN: this is a great trick. Use it wisely.

SB10BEN: OK, I gotta run. Dev meeting in 5.

OBenwhY: Wait! I thought we were going to test ways to milk fairy tears today.

OBenwhY: i brought a fairy trap i made all by myself

SB10BEN: Sorry. I got distracted by giving you superpowers.

SB10BEN: Next time, I promise.

SB10BEN: You can stick around and harass fairies by yourself, if you want.

SB10BEN: or blow stuff up. Either way.

OBenwhY: it's not as fun without you, but fiiiiine.

SB10BEN: Smell ya later, crocodile.

OBenwhY: After a while, chimichanga.

OBenwhY: Thanks for the earbuds!

OBenwhY: and the maybe not-super-great advice!

SB10BEN HAS EXITED GAME

OBenwhY HAS EXITED GAME

SCHOOL

It's fine.
It's fine.
It's fine.
It's fine.
It's fine.
It's fine.
It's fine.
It's fine.
It's fine.

▫ ▫ ▫ ▫

Whoaaaaaa.
Check out Ben Who What Why!
Hey, Ben Who What Why, who is your hairstylist?
Hey, Ben Who What Why, what ARE you—I mean, what
were you thinking?
Hey, Ben Who What Whyyyyy don't you ask Dress Code
for a wig to borrow?

▫ ▫ ▫ ▫

Ignore it.
Chin up.
Shoulders back.
Eyes forward.

Work it.
Flaunt it.
Own it.

□ □ □ □

Sleek.
Cool.
Almost scary.

Sleek.
Cool
Almost scary.

I'll keep repeating
all of this
in my head
until I believe it.

Will I ever believe it?

□ □ □ □

Will Ace ever believe it?

□ □ □ □

Is Ace even *at* school?

I haven't heard
Mr. Mann shout
DRESS CODE
even once today.

□ □ □ □

Hey, Ben Who What Whyyyyy did you shave your head,
    for attention?
Why, Ben Who What Why? We already pay you a LOT
    of attention.
Okay, Ben Who What Why, if that's what you who-what-want.
Challenge accepted!

□ □ □ □

I'm used to the comments.

They started when my brother died,
but those were different—
whispery,
far away,
like I had a disease
no one wanted to catch.

The comments changed
when I changed;
when I started to dress
and look
and feel
and *be*
Ben
instead of the Benita
everyone thought
they knew.

There are a lot of Bens in school,
so I can't just be Ben,
I have to be Ben Y,
which is like a gift
to everyone
who wants to know
Ben WHY, did you change your name?
Ben WHO do you think you are?
Ben WHAT are you . . . trying to say?
Ben Who What Whyyyyy are you so . . . weird?

I'm used to hearing it all.
I try not to care.
Because I know
I know
even if I have dead-brother-itis,

even if I changed my name,
even if my existence
causes more questions
than answers,
I know
if I try hard enough,
I can pretend I don't care,
I can pretend
I'm too cool
for school.

On a good day,
at least.

▫ ▫ ▫ ▫

The problem is,
today is not a good day.

Hair is somehow . . .
different.
I can't explain how,
it just is.

So today?
I can't pretend I don't care.
I can't pretend I don't hear.
I can't pretend

I'm too cool
for school
because
my heart pounds loud,
my throat is closed off,
squeezing
a permanent rock,
and I can't
stop
sweating,
even though I'm trying,
I really am,
to own it.

I'm trying,
I'm trying,
I'm trying,
but . . .

▫ ▫ ▫ ▫

Uh.
Ace is at my locker.
Right there.
Pink hair today,
chin-length,
camo jacket,
army boots,

and it occurs to me
this might not be cosplay at all.
Maybe it's just Ace being Ace?
But how could I really know that
without knowing *Ace* at all?
and without knowing
any of the comics or books
with the characters people want to become.

An idea strikes me,
out of place for right now,
for this day,
for this time,
that maybe
reading a book
(here and there)
might give you a reason
to talk to someone
(here and there)
and maybe THAT is a reason
people read stuff
like, for fun—

but then the thought is gone
when Ace opens the locker next to mine,
looks at me,
says:
I traded with that kid.
You know the one with the . . .
extra face-like face?
Anyway.
I like to move lockers
every few weeks.
Keep Mr. Mann
on his toes.
If he can't find me,
no DRESS CODE!
That's my theory,
at least.
It hasn't worked yet,
but maybe this locker
is the key.

Then Ace bows,
like we just,
I don't know,
finished dancing
or something,
and says:

Nice hair,

before slamming the locker door
and bouncing off
down the hall.

▫ ▫ ▫ ▫

Five seconds later
I hear *DRESS CODE!*
echo around the corner
and I wonder:
Where will Ace's locker be
tomorrow?

▫ ▫ ▫ ▫

Jordan's Muppet arms flail
around me,
toward me,
at me,
while I attempt
to figure out
exactly
what just happened.

Was Ace complimenting me?
Or teasing me?
Or—

You look super fierce. You really do! Doesn't she look fierce?

Ben B and Javier
appear
out of nowhere,
like no one told me
my locker
is a teleporter
now.

We had an accidental adventure last night and when I went home, I was feeling some feelings about the whole thing, but now you look like a movie star who saves everyone at the end of the world and I'm feeling WAY better feelings unless it's ACTUALLY the end of the world, in which case please save me first so you can have a hilarious sidekick who dances like there's LITERALLY no tomorrow. But also save Ben B and Javier because we can't live without them.

□ □ □ □

It's . . . wow.
It's . . . do you want to talk about it?
Or . . .

Ben B.
Carefully choosing the words he needs,
deleting the ones he doesn't,
watching him try to talk right now
is like watching him type:
He wants so badly to get it right
but sometimes all of his trying
stops him from getting it
at all.

▫ ▫ ▫ ▫

Javier.
Master of the five-second sketch.
He always seems to know *exactly* what to say,
without saying anything
at all.

□ □ □ □

Ben B, Javier, Jordan
disappear into the crowd,
on their way to class.

It's not the first time
or the last
that I'll wish
we all shared
every class
and that every class
was in room 113
under the stairs.

□ □ □ □

I try not to hear the whispers
or the shouts
as everyone sees me
pushing my way through the crowds,
trying to get to class fast
for maybe the first time ever.

Ms. J stands in the library doorway,
hollering at kids to walk,
and to watch where they're going,
and to pick up stuff they drop.

She sees me walk by,
I see her see me walk by.

She opens her mouth,
but stays frozen
for just one hot second
like she can't find
the right words
to holler in my direction.

I shake my head
to let her know
I don't need her to shout anything,
I don't need her help pointing me out
in the jostling crowd.

But she has a successful reboot,
and the words shoot
from her mouth,
loud, clear,
sailing at me
across the hall:

Surprising but divine sartorial choice today, Ben Y!
Can't wait to see you later at—

She tries to wink
but just blinks
both eyes
together
at the same time,
omg.

Newspaper Typing Club!

And seriously,
she is so
embarrassing,
I just *can't even*
with any part of her
right now
or probably even later
at Newspaper Typing Club,

and ugh.
Everything is . . .
ugh.

I just can't.

She continues to shout:

Sartorial means clothes!
I like your outfit!
That's all I'm talking about!

And then she tries to wink again,
so I shout: *I know what it means!*
even though I have never heard
the word *sartorial*
ever in my life
until right now.

□ □ □ □

It took all summer,
but Ben B, Jordan, Javier
and I . . .
we worked REALLY hard
to get Ms. J polished and trained.

She used books and forest-bathing
to teach us
it's okay to be divergent learners,
and we used virtual building blocks
to teach *her*
how to teach *us*
to trust her.

We sorted out
(even celebrated)
her piles of mean-wells,
even her full-on mistakes,
until we created
the number-one best
teacher-friend-Sandbox-playing person
that any of us
had ever had.

When she got reassigned
(which, yeah, was totally our fault)
((but also hers too!)),
I wasn't sure if she could stay
as fun and weird and cool and different
with her new librarian job,
working in the one place at school
none of us ever ever ever
wants to go.

But then she created
Typing Club,
which was really
*Everyone, Even Ms. J, Plays Sandbox Together After School
in the Library Club. . . .*
And even when Mr. Mann
stormed into the library,
interrupting Typing Club
(after he found out
Typing Club was really
*Everyone, Even Ms. J, Plays Sandbox Together After School
in the Library Club*),
and he huffed and puffed
in Ms. J's office
until she promised
we would type stuff
Of Substance
in Typing Club. . . .

Even when she
announced
*Everyone, Even Ms. J, Plays Sandbox Together After School
in the Library Club*
had become *Everyone, Even Ms. J, Types Stuff Of Substance
Club, aka: Newspaper Typing Club). . . .*

EVEN THEN,
I knew.
Yeah.
She's still
a divergent thinker,
just like she describes us
(the kids from room 113)
(the kids under the stairs).
She's still the same Ms. J.
Still fun and weird and cool and different.
Still getting in trouble
(almost)
as much as we do.
And she's maybe the only reason
other than Ben B, Jordan, and Javier
that I don't haaaaaaaaaate
coming to school every day.

Even if some days,
brainstorming Substance
has to come before
melting ghosts.

□ □ □ □

I finally make it to class,
finally slide into my seat.
I jam my hands into my pockets,
And . . .

I smile,
shaking out
the tangled-up
earbuds
hiding in my pocket.

My invisibility cloak.
I pop them in, because really,
I never give up
the ridiculous hope that,
like Sandbox,
they can make the impossible
possible,
and *poof*
I'll be *actually* invisible
for once.

◻ ◻ ◻ ◻

Why is Ben Who What Why so . . . like that?
Like, helloooo, if Ben Who What Why tried any harder?
She'd turn into Dress Code.
And what why who would want to look like THAT?

Shhhh! Annabelle! She's right there. What if she hears you?
She can't hear me. Look at those ugly earbuds!
You can see them from space.
Too bad she can't hear me, though.
She could use my fashion advice right now.
So could Dress Code.

▫ ▫ ▫ ▫

It's been a really long week
and it isn't even lunch yet.

▫ ▫ ▫ ▫

Hear me out. . . .
Let's grab our lunches,
take them to the library,
say hey to Ms. J,
maybe eat fast,
sneak in some Sandbox?

Ben B might not be saying,
Let's protect you from whatever
hideous hideousness awaits
in the stewing stink
of the cafeteria
out loud,
but I can tell it's what he means.

Probably the lunchroom is going to be a stewing stink today.
I mean, not just a literal stewing stink, like it is every day,
but also the kind of stewing stink that's made of eyeballs and
whispers and is stirred around by the kind of people my mom
says shouldn't matter and don't matter, even though somehow
they have decided that they are the only people who do matter.

Clearly,
Jordan is reading my mind,
and also clearly,
Ben B and Jordan
do not have to be
invisible
at all
to hear the
constant *blah blah* hum,
the *Ben Y* this and *Benita* that
the *chatter chatter chatter chatter*
nonstop
echoing
through the halls.

▫ ▫ ▫ ▫

You look older and taller.
Quite severe, actually,
but in a good way.
Like a Roman bust come to life.
I love it!

Ms. J offers her take
before I barely have two feet
in the library
and jeez,
isn't she breaking
the most important librarian rule
by shouting at me like that
from the other side of the room?
Why is she always so *loud*?

□ ⊔ □ ◻

Fine. Sure.
Sometimes I like it that she's loud.

I like how her voice
and her hair
and her caftans
and her . . . self
can take over a whole room,
a whole *library*.

But sometimes I don't like it.
Sometimes meaning right now.

□ □ □ □

You're quiet today, Ben Y.
Part of your new severeness?

Ms. J's voice,
still loud,
rises and falls
over our lunches,
over the crunching and slurping,
over Ben B's story
about soccer practice,
over Jordan's descriptions
of my hair falling out,
over me,
over me,
over me.

Her eyes . . .
they do that thing they do
when they can see right through
my guts
and I know

the little joking bend in her voice
is just for show
because her eyes . . .
they hold me tight,
and they seem
just the tiniest,
smidge-i-est
worried.

I let her eyes hold mine.
For just a second,
before I look away.

I shrug.

She squeezes my shoulder
super fast
before she stands up,
and I can smell her cloud
of very light
and already tired
perfume.

Ten minutes left
before the bell.
Shall we attempt a little . . .

She just cannot wink
to save her life.
It makes my heart smile
maybe for the first time today.

She finishes her question
by loud-whispering,
Newspaper Typing Club,
minus the Newspaper part?

And we all jump up
and run
to the computers.

□ □ □ □

I start to feel
almost
kind of
maybe
okay
ish.

□ □ □ □

Ben B laughs
when Jordan jumps up,
wiggling and flailing

to some weird music
Ms. J says is
calming
and
meditative
and
perfect for creating.

Too bad Javi has B lunch.
I'd like to see his drawing
of whatever it is
you're doing.

Jordan rolls his eyes
toward Ben B
in a very
non calm
way.

I'm doing a thing called dancing, Ben B. Ever heard of it?
You let your whole body listen to a song and then your whole
body tells you what the song is about by moving around.

Oh, that's what it's called.
I thought maybe
some fire ants
crawled in your pants.

I would like to point out,
Ms. J says,
without looking up
from her computer,
There is no talking
or dancing
in Typing Club,
even if it's minus
the Newspaper part.

I would like to point out this is technically lunchtime and
not technically Newspaper Typing Club or any kind of Typing
Club at all, and also that you are technically playing dancing
music, Ms. J.

Now Ms. J looks up.

I would like to point out
you, sir, are technically
on thin ice.

Her halfway smile
is also a halfway
GOTCHA,
and Jordan sits back down
with a small

grouchy
fart noise
and a halfway smile
of his own.

□ □ □ □

I bet, if he were here,
Javier's hand would hurt
after drawing all of this.

For a second,
I wonder if he's *glad*
he has B lunch.
But nah.
No one's *glad* to have B lunch.
They run out of pizza halfway through.
Plus, we're not there
to make his hand hurt
from drawing
all our dumb stuff.

*Plus*plus, he's missing out
on spontaneous
Not Newspaper, Yes Typing Club,
which must be a huge bummer,

even with
calming
and
meditative
(so-called) *music.*

□ □ □ □

An announcement,
loud and crackly,
bounces down
from the ceiling speakers,
drowning out
Ms. J's
supposedly calming
music.

Hellooooooooooo,
Hart ROCKETS!
I couldn't WAIT
for tomorrow morning
to announce this SURPRISE!
I'm positively BLASTING OFF
with good NEWS!

Ugh.
Mr. Mann.
Anything that gets him

this excited?
It has to be
baaaaaaad news.

Hart Middle SCHOOL!

We can hear him breathing
into the microphone.

[loud exhale]

Has been OFFICIALLY approved!

[loud inhale]

To join IN!
The National!
ZERO-Tolerance!
ANTI-Bullying!

[loud inhale]

Planet Safe SPACE CAMPAIGN!

[loud exhale]

More details FORTHCOMING
in the FIRST edition
of our own REVIVED

school newspaper,
the Hart TIMES!

Uh. WHAT?
We all stare at the ceiling speakers,
but no explanations crackle out.
Only Mr. Mann's voice,
still booming:

ALL boys and girls will SOON get a chance
To FUEL UP!
With KINDNESS!
And BLAST OFF!
To Planet SAFE SPACE!
ToGETHER!

[pause]

Participation
is mandatory.

▫ ▫ ▫ ▫

I can feel my face
twist in a confused knot
as I mutter,

Am I the only one
who thinks
Mr. Mann
is the only human
in the history of humans
to make kindness
seem like something . . .
annoying?

Jordan nods,
very seriously,
and says,
Maybe because he's such a . . .

I say:

Jerk?

at the same time
Jordan says:

Turd?

And we both
bust out laughing.

A JERD!
Jordan giggles.
We just made that up, Ben Y! And it is the truest truth ever.
Mr. Mann is SUCH a jerd!
Jordan pauses
for a super-quick
half of a half second
before his face crinkles,
and he says, confused:

What even is a space campaign?

▫ ▫ ▫ ▫

Ms. J
is so bad
at trying not to laugh
and trying to be mad,
but she tries anyway.

And when her face
does the thing?
Where her eyes chuckle?
But her mouth
frowns?

It fills me up
with little bubbles
that explode behind my nose
and make me snort.

(And then I snort more
when she gets
(not) mad
about that, too.)

▫ ▫ ▫ ▫

When I stop snorting,
I start talking,
because, yeah,
I have a lot of questions now
(just like always).

Here's a question
for everyone in this room
who's smarter than me,
which might be everyone:

(Ms. J tosses me a look
that says, *Oh come on,*
you know you're smart.

And I admit,
maybe
I said the thing
about not being smart
just so I could see that look
and tuck it away
to remember later.)

I pretend like I *don't* see
that look, though,
because no way
do I want Ms. J
to know
I think about the things
she tells me
with her eyes
(and even her face).
That would be . . .
ugh . . .
super embarrassing.

I look up at the ceiling,
as if it has all the answers.

Why do we have to
BLAST OFF
to Planet *Safe Space?*

Like, you already blast off into space, *right?*
Why do you need to blast off to
Planet *Safe Space?*
Why can't you just blast off
into space that is . . . safe?
You know?
Blast off into Safe Space?
Doesn't that make more sense?

Ms. J's mouth opens,
but I keep talking,
because my questions
make me think
of new questions.

And another question . . .
Who exactly
is writing about this
in the Hart Times?
We have our assignments already,
so . . . ?

Everyone stares at me.

ALSO! What if you're not a boy or a girl?
Are you not invited to Planet Safe Space?

Those are . . .
a lot of great questions.

Ms. J's words slide together,
like she's piecing together
the puzzle, too.

I'm sure Mr. Mann means
all genders are welcome.
Her crinkled face doesn't look very sure, though.

As for the Hart Times *article . . .*
She shrugs.
No earthly idea what that's about.

And really interesting point,
about Safe Space
minus the Planet part.
Great observation, Ben Y.

She puts her hand up for a high five.
But is this really
a high five
kind of moment?

Sometimes
Ms. J is so dorky,
it almost

actually
hurts
to be near her.

▫ ▫ ▫ ▫

There's a blur,
then a smacking sound
as Ms. J staggers back
before standing straight again
and out of nowhere,
Ace is here,
out of breath,
gasping,

Never—
leave—
a high five
hanging—

Ace's pink wig
is crooked
from the sudden running
and jumping
and high-fiving.

Ace's smile is
also crooked
as it fades
almost as fast
as Ms. J's smile did
one (post–high five)
second ago.

I'm sorry . . .
did you just RUN *across this library?*
Did you just SMACK ME *unannounced?*
Ms. J sucks in both of her lips,
turning her mouth into a line
that looks a lot like
the deep line
forming across
her Very Concerned
forehead.

Ace swallows hard,
adjusts the wig,
seems to need
a search party
to find the shining smile
from a second ago,

and in this flash,
I see something familiar
instead of fancy and new.

I see a kid in combat boots,
wearing a dirty pink wig,
and panicking
because
a teacher
just snatched control
of the moment
in a snap,
draining away
any power of surprise
Ace may have had.

In this second,
Ms. J does not—
repeat—
does not
think Ace
is acting cute
at all.

And Ace's face
in this second
looks like
how I've felt
in my guts
many, many times
when I did a thing
or said a thing
I wished I'd thought about
first.

◦ ◦ ◦ ◦

I'm sorry . . .
Ms. J says again,
staring daggers at Ace.
Her arms cross,
squeezing her chest,
which is never
ever
a good sign.

WHAT *is your name?*

Ace shifts
from one combat boot
to the other,

and scratches
quickly
at the wig.

I'm Ace.

Ms. J nods,
looks at me for some reason,
looks back at Ace,
says:

It's nice to meet you, Ace.
Please never do
any
of the things
you just did
in this library
ever again.

It's Ace's turn to nod.

Now Ms. J's whole self smiles
along with her face
as she says,
Excellent.
And then,
Welcome to the library, Ace.
Talk to me about the books you're reading right now.

The two of them walk off together
like they are brand-new
best friends,
but not before Ace
tosses a grin at me,
like it's an over-the-shoulder
Frisbee fling,
and WHY
is everyone looking at ME?

□ □ □ □

Oh right.
Bald head.
I forgot for a second.

□ □ □ □

Except.
Ace's Frisbee-fling grin
wasn't a bald-head look.
And Ms. J's
quick-stop glance
wasn't a bald-head look.
So . . .
What?

□ □ □ □

I watch them go,
and the more I think about it,
the more I know for sure:

Ace is a *Me*.
And I am an Ace.

I know it from a deep-down place,
where you know things
because you *feel* them,
not because you learn them.

I know.
I just do.

▫ ▫ ▫ ▫

You know in your guts
what you know,
you know?

You know what scares you.
You know what makes you laugh.
You know what you like.
You know what you don't.
You know *who* you like.
You know who you don't.

And sometimes
you see someone
or meet someone
and you hear a little
ping
in your heart,
and you know,
just like that,
this is someone
who's like *you*,
boom.

You can't explain how you know
because there's nothing *to* explain.

You know in your guts
what you know,
you know?

◻ ◻ ◻ ◻

I've never had the right words—
to describe what I know
about myself,
other than by describing
what I know I'm *not*.

I'm not like him,
I'm not like her,
I'm not like anyone
I've ever known
or met
or seen
at school.

So, somehow,
just as much
as I know
I'm *not* like him
or her
or anyone else at school,
I *do* know,
from deep down
in the place
where you know
deep-down truths:

If Ace is a me
and I am an Ace
then that means
I'm not just
a *not* someone
anymore.

Even if we don't
really know
each other,
and even if we aren't
technically friends,
it's still a surprising,
out-of-nowhere feeling
of . . . relief, maybe?
To know I'm not alone.

There are two of us now.

And it doesn't matter
if we're friends
or if we aren't,
because two is still two.

Two is not nothing.

Two feels so much better
than none.

▫ ▫ ▫ ▫

The bell beeps its ring,
and my stomach sinks
because that means
back into the belly
of the Hart Middle beast.

◦ ◦ ◦ ◦

I'll figure out what Mr. Mann meant!

Ms. J shouts across the library
as Jordan, Ben B, and I
head toward the door,
dragging our feet,
moving slow.

About the Planet Safe Space article, I mean!
See you y'alls later!

Ace,
still at her side,
holding a stack of books now,
shifts the stack
to one pink-clad hip,
smiles that sparkling
fresh-mint smile,
and waves.

Yeah, see you y'alls later!

Jordan and Ben B
side-eye me
as we slide out the door
and Jordan says,
You y'alls is our *thing.*

I know what Jordan means, but . . .
technically?
Ace seems made to be a you y'all.
Just like me.

I don't say anything
because I've been swallowed
by the laughs streaming my way
in the crowded hallway,
and it takes
my whole
entire
concentrating
ability
(which is,
admittedly,
not the best)
to drown out
all the comments
so that I don't just . . .
drown.

< NEWSPAPER TYPING CLUB CHAT >

JJ11347: Can I have some help over here?

JJ11347: We need to get started on the shelves for the poetry section.

OBenwhY: BenBee has some good building skillz.

JJ11347: "Skills," Ben Y. You know that. Proper grammar in Typing Club.

OBenwhY: 😦

BenBee: but my skills are so good, they're skillzzzz!

JJ11347: 😦

JORDANJMAGEDDON!!!!!: I built some shelves out of chickens once.

BenBee: Seems like we've worked on the library enough for today.

BenBee: Maybe I can use my building skills(z) doing something else?

JJ11347: None of you have done ANY work today, BenBee.

JJ11347: You all literally just got here and ate a snack. That's it.

JJ11347: jajajavier:)! Stop blowing up chickens!

JJ11347: Look what you did to the rug OBenwhY added. Gross!

JORDANJMAGEDDON!!!!: Javi! How am I supposed to make my chicken shelves???

jajajavier:): if i can't blow up chickens, i'll have to change my avatar name to jajajavier:(

BenBee: Why are we even building a library, again?

BenBee: IN A VIDEO GAME??

BenBee: Does Sandbox really need one?

JJ11347: You hurt my heart, BenBee, when you say things like that.

Ms. J leans back in her chair,
her gold and turquoise caftan
shimmering around her,
as she breaks the number-one
most important rule
of Newspaper Typing Club:
No Talking during the Typing Club part.

You know,
there are
entire
undiscovered
universes
in libraries, right?

She flings her arms
out to her sides
like she's about to
shoot fireworks
from her fingertips.

Jordan snickers,
but one look from Ms. J
stops his snickers
only halfway
out of his nose.

Worlds, realms, lifetimes—
You would never get to experience
ANY of it
ANYwhere else!
And it's all right here!
In the real library!

She drops her arms,
scooches her chair
closer to her computer,
and starts to type
louder than usual:

JJ11347: It only makes sense that you should find THAT kind of magic,

JJ11347: if not even *more incredible* magic, in a Sandbox library.

She looks up
over the top
of her monitor,
and somehow
her *eyes* frown
right at the edges,
not hiding
the little bit of sad
sneaking out.
She looks back down.

JJ11347: That's why I thought it would be awesome for us to do this together.

JJ11347: Because libraries are magic, and Sandbox is magic

JJ11347: and I know you y'alls are so good at making magic.

JJ11347: But fine. Save the shelves for another time.

JJ11347: Go get your notebooks.

BenBee: 😒 Thanks a lot Javier

jajajavier:): what?? I didn't do anything! You're the one being mean to libraries!

jajajavier:): which are totally awesome and full of awesome things. 😊

JJ11347: Enough. Everyone go get your notebooks.

OBenwhY: any news about the , Ms. J?

JJ11347: Nothing yet. But I left several messages for Mr. Mann.

👾 👾 👾 👾

Hey.

We all look up
as Ace wanders over,
and wow
Ace seems to be . . .
everywhere
these days.

Ace gives a little bow,
dropping a bursting backpack
BAM,
on my table,
half landing on my keyboard,
making it go AZXCCCCCCCCCCCCCCCCCCCCCCCCCCCC
in chat
until I get a chat infraction
AND ANOTHER ONE
until I yank the keyboard away,
clutching it to my chest,
hitting GGGGGGGGGGGGGGGGGGGGGGGGGGGGG
until I get my third chat infraction
in, like, five seconds
and get ejected from the game.

Ace looks up from the giant backpack,
waving a wrinkled paper,

grinning that shiny, sparkly,
24-carat-gold
stupid-cute grin.

Can someone show me
how to find bus . . . uh . . .

Ace looks down,
squints at the paper.

. . . 315?
My grandma can't pick me up today
and blah blah blah. . . .

Ms. J points at me, smiles.

Ben Y can show you how to find the 315.
She knows everything about the buses!

I give her a look like, *What??*
What kind of dink knows everything about the buses??

I find some words that say:

Like, show Ace right now?
But aren't we about to,
uh—
start newspapering?

Ace's laugh
reminds me of
the smoothing rough
skritch skritch noise
of sandpaper
if sandpaper
could whisper.

I didn't know
newspapering
was a verb.

Ace looks up,
thinking.

Or a gerund?

Ms. J's eyes
almost
actually
turn into hearts
as she says:

Forget the 315.
Ace, would you like
to join Newspaper Typing Club?

And, oh boy . . .
I can practically hear
the wildly swiveling eyeballs
of Ben B, Javier, and Jordan
as they all swing their eyes
to Ms. J
and silently scream:
HANG ON.
WHAT.

▫ ▫ ▫ ▫

Ace shrugs
in such an easy way,
such a smooth movement,
I'm convinced
for a second
that Ace invented
shrugging.

Gotta ask my grandma, I guess.
And if she says yes,
I might be late
most of the time,
because, uh,
I have detention
like four times a week
for the rest of my life.

Ms. J says,
That's a lot of detentions.

Ace shrugs again.
My fabulous style breaks a LOT of rules.
According to Mr. Mann
Supreme Overlord of DRESS CODE enforcement.

Ace twists a rainbow earring
staring off into space for a second, then
blinks back to Earth, saying,

I do still have to find the 315, though.
Like, right now?
I have to be home, stat.

Ms. J breaks into my thoughts,
snapping her fingers with each word:

Ben Y.
Please.
The 315.

▫ ▫ ▫ ▫

So here we are.
Side by side.
Walking to the 315.
Long stride matching long stride.

I want to fill the spaces
between our strides
with all the questions
that have popped to mind:

You know what a gerund is, huh?
When did you move to Freshwater?
Where did you move from?
Do you really have THAT many detentions?
You live with your grandma?

But somehow,
I manage to keep quiet
for once
while I think of things to say
that aren't questions
and that Ace might think
are cool or—

Shorter strides
pound behind us
and Jordan catches up,
already explaining,

—and I said I'll be right back I just want to make sure no
one gets lost or anything plus also it'll be good research for
my article about the importance of cardio fitness for kids
who—who—

he puts his hands on his knees,
leans forward,
huffing and puffing

—*play too many video games.*

Jordan looks up,
smiles.

Hi. Good. You don't seem lost.

I give him my best
what in the world? look,
but he ignores me,
linking elbows with Ace
as they walk ahead.

*I have an important question for you, Ace, Did you ever
see that old movie about a pet detective named Ace? It's
a really terrible movie, which makes me wonder why your
parents would name you after someone in it? Unless they
didn't? Unless you're an actual pet detective? And they
always have to be named Ace? Sorry, that was more than
one important question.*

Ace's eyebrows falter in a way
I've seen before
when people meet Jordan,

like they aren't sure
if he's joking
or if he's sincere
or if Jordan is making fun of them
or if they should be making fun of *him*.

I am not a pet detective.
Not named after one, either.
So, you're zero for two there, big guy.

And now Ace is trying to catch my eye,
I can feel it,
so we can share a wink-wink, eyebrow-waggle,
what's-up-with-this-weirdo-Jordan joke.

But nope.
I don't do Jordan jokes.
Ever.
At all.
Not even when he's being
extra strange
like he is
right now.

There's the 315.

I say it quickly,
interrupting Jordan
before he can launch into
a whole thing
about some other thing
that only Jordan
would launch into.

It's right there.

I point to the city bus
already stopped
at the end of the block.

Better run.

That's it?
Oh, crud!

Ace takes off running.

Jordan links arms with me now,
as we turn around
and jog together
back to school.

▫ ▫ ▫ ▫

What was that all about?

I unlink my arm
and turn around,
jogging backward,
so I can face Jordan.

What was what?

Jordan shrugs
and it's such the opposite
of Ace's smooth-move shrug,
it fills me
with the warm-squishy feeling
that comes from
knowing someone
so well,
you can tell
their squirrely shrug
means they know
exactly
what was what.

Jordan stops jogging.
I stop, too.

*You make me nervous when you jog backward Ben Y because
what if there's a sinkhole you can't see and you fall in it? And
actually, huh, that's interesting, I think Ace kind of gives me
the same feeling I get when I'm worried about you not seeing
a sinkhole and falling in. Does that make any sense at all?
Probably not. All I know is something about that kid crinkles
my stomach in a WATCH OUT FOR SINKHOLES kind of
way even though my brain keeps reminding me that Ace seems
fine and nice. It's like my stomach and my brain are arguing
which maybe doesn't make a lot of sense but is the best way
I can think of to explain why I ran after you.*

Fair enough,
I say,
and then after a minute,

*Sinkholes are really big, you know.
I'd see the warning
in your big yikes eyes
if one was behind me.*

□ □ □ □

For the rest of the afternoon,
I work on my article
about the value
and awesomeness
of shopping

at thrift stores,
while I steal glances
at Jordan,
who seems to be acting
maybe
just a little bit
stranger
than usual.

Most of the time
I can figure out
everything Jordan is thinking,
sometimes even before
Jordan knows
what he's thinking,
but right now,
based on his forehead wrinkles
and his not-smile
but not-frown,
I can't figure it out.

Maybe he's having trouble
with his cardio article,
or maybe he's still worrying
Ace might be a sinkhole
I could fall into.

Huh.

OBenwhY: Hi again.

OBenwhY: in case you were wondering, yes, i am still bald

OBenwhY: in case you were also wondering, yes, school WAS *that* bad

OBenwhY: also, earbud invisibility is not nearly as useful as actual invisibility

OBenwhY: though it does kind of muffle the mean voices

OBenwhY: and that's better than nothing

OBenwhY: i guess

OBenwhY: not really

OBenwhY: anyway

OBenwhY: . . .

OBenwhY: how was your day?

OBenwhY: are you very busy now? Doing ghosty things?

OBenwhY: do you get to watch over all of us? in all our separate places all day?

OBenwhY: . . .

OBenwhY: Seems like that would be kind of terrible, actually

OBenwhY: I mean, why watch us if you can't help out in any way?

OBenwhY: and obviously you can't help us, right?

OBenwhY: because you would if you could, right?

OBenwhY: like pull the fire alarm to save me from a pop quiz?

OBenwhY: or flood the locker room to cancel gym class?

OBenwhY: . . .

OBenwhY: ugh

OBenwhY: . . .

OBenwhY: did you see that Ace kid today?

OBenwhY: when you were watching over me but not helping?

OBenwhY: i wish you could help me figure out if I want Ace to be my friend

OBenwhY: i mean, i *think* I do? But also . . .

OBenwhY: Ace is kind of . . . a lot?

OBenwhY: Also also, for some reason it feels important for Ace to think *I'm* cool?

OBenwhY: even though I know I can *also* be . . . a lot?

OBenwhY: I know. None of that makes much sense. That's why I need your help.

OBenwhY: that's why now is the perfect chance for you to wave a wand or send a sign

OBenwhY: . . .

OBenwhY: Anything?

OBenwhY: . . .

OBenwhY: no advice at all? really?

0BenwhY: . . .

0BenwhY: that's so unlike you, Benicio.

0BenwhY: . . .

0BenwhY: As you would say, this has been a delight, but I really do have to go now.

0BenwhY: smell ya later, ghost breath

HOME

I rock back and forth
squeak squeak squeak
and I can almost match
my heartbeat *beat beat*
while I sit in Benicio's chair
at Benicio's old desk
in Benicio's old room
and think think think
about nothing
and everything
and how he used to tell me
how all this school stuff,
how all this kid stuff
feels like it's everything
like it powers your breath
and your guts
and all your feelings
and it feeds you
and makes you sick
and it's so much everything
and how you think you can't escape.

But you can,
he'd say.
You will, kiddo.
Trust me.
You'll pull yourself free
from the middle-school ooze,
and when you do?
You'll still be you,
but you'll be a new you.
You'll realize all this stuff,
all these swallowing everythings . . .
they're nothing,
in the grand scheme of life.
Or at least,
they're nothing
in the grand scheme
of growing up
and getting out
and seeing how big the world is
outside of the only ooze
you've ever known.

How is it
that I can't remember my Earth Science assignments,
and I can't remember articles versus prepositions,
but I will never forget,
ever,

in a million billion years,
Benicio's words
from that time he taught me
everything is really nothing
and *that* is the thing
I should hold on to.
That is the thing
I should look forward to
the most.

□ □ □ □

Dinner is ready, Mr. Clean!

Mom's voice echoes down the hall,
along with Esme's giggle.

Great.
Just what I need.
Mom's a comedian now?

A tiny smile fights its way
to the tiniest corner
of my mouth.

At least that joke means
she's here with us tonight,

instead of lost
in her thoughts
like every other night.

It means she's opened
her usually tired,
usually sighing,
usually closed,
eyes,
and she's *seen* me.

But also?
It means she's *thought* about me
long enough
to make a joke.
You can't make a joke
if you aren't paying attention,
at least a little bit.

And if Mom's paying attention?
To me?
Even if it's a little bit?
I'll take it.

▫ ▫ ▫ ▫

So.

Mom leans over her plate,
sawing her knife
back and forth,
back and forth,
like she's getting revenge
on a chicken thigh
that treated her wrong.

How did your—

she waves her hand at me
like a magician
trying to make a rabbit
disappear—

this—
work out today?

Esme blows her giggle
through her straw
making giant
gross
milk bubbles.

Great,
my voice says,
ahead of my brain,
as usual.
Really awesome
and great.
Greater than you'd think.

The idea
of reliving this day
out loud
in detail
so that Mom and Esme
can laugh about it . . .

The idea
that my awful day
could make their day
funnier and better
makes my guts bubble
with rage.

In fact,
I've changed my mind.
I actually DON'T want Mom

to open her tired eyes
to notice me
or see me
or anything
if this
is what will happen.

IT WAS GREAT.

My heart pounds so hard
I'm afraid it might
shake loose
the tears
I've hidden
on the highest shelves
in the darkest corners
of myself
all day today.

Mom swallows
the last bite
of her chicken,
looks up,
and says:

You already said that, mija.
But what made it so great?

Her eyebrows are high,
expecting more words
to escape from me.

Esme's big eyes peer
over her teetering milk bubbles
as the bubbles threaten to drip
and slide
down the side
of her glass.

One bubble
has had enough,
and the slimy white goop
breaks loose,
a cascading escape
rushing to create
a puddle
on the table,
messy
and gross,
and for some reason
that broken bubble
breaks me, too,
and my gross mess
starts to drip
and slide

from my nose and eyes
as I stand up,
choke out the words:

Everything, okay.
Everything made it great.

And I make it to the bathroom
just in time
to turn on the shower,
to see the last remnants
of yesterday's hair
make a mucky swirl
in the still-cold water,
just in time
to drown out
the heaving
hiccupping cries
bubbling over
after my
really great
and awesome
day
at school.

▫ ▫ ▫ ▫

When I leave the bathroom,
Mom's bedroom door is shut
and that means no knocking
unless there is blood
or guts
or more than one barf.

When I get to my room
(which is also Esme's room,
which is never not annoying
because there's a room
right there
across the hall
that could be MY room
and MY room alone,
but it never will be,
so uuuggghhh) . . .

when I get to OUR room,
Esme is in her bunk
humming a song
I'm pretty sure she made up
with the highest of high notes
and the lowest of low notes
and the thought crosses my mind
for the millionth time

that maybe Esme is
actually
half bird, half girl.

She leans her head
over the edge
of her bed
so she can look up
at me
as I climb the steps
to my bunk,
and her bird voice
chirps:

Are you okay?
Is everything still great?

I fling myself into bed,
my bald head sliding
across my pillow,
bonking into
the metal bed frame
with a clang
as deep as a church bell's
on a funeral day.

A-OK,
I say.
And then . . .
Ow.

Ow,
Esme echoes.

And then she goes back to her song,
humming quietly
until we both
fall asleep.

SCHOOL

Beige is a color, sure.
It blandly blends,
and it blends blandly.
It isn't happy.
It isn't sad.
It's just . . . beige.

There has always been beige.
There will always be beige.
It is what it is.
Because it's beige.

But beige isn't just a color.
Beige is also
a state of mind.

Embrace the beige
so you can blend blandly,
and blandly blend;
so you can join
the one big Everyone
that fills the halls
like a soggy glob
stuck in a throat,

that can't be coughed out
no matter how hard
you try.

There has always been beige.
There will always be beige.
It is what it is.
Because it's beige.

And if you don't embrace it?
If you don't easily blend?
Beige tries to swallow YOU whole—
or worse, you've already been devoured
and you don't even know.

◦ ◦ ◦ ◦

The beige has this way
of seeping into your brain,
of making you wonder—
if there's so many of *them*,
and not very many of *you*,
maybe
just maybe
you *are* wrong or bad
for not fitting
into the blob,

and maybe
just maybe
the safety
of being the same
is better than
the danger
of being you.

▫ ▫ ▫ ▫

When I climb the steps
to the front door of school,
I can barely squeeze through;
the glob of beige
feels particularly chokey today.

At the edge of the glob
I hear laughing,
and as I push my way around,
the laughing gets louder
and my stomach drops
and I feel my head go light
from surprise
because I see why the blob is laughing.
Standing out
in the sea of beige is:

Ace.

Ace, wearing a see-from-space
orange poncho
with the words
DRESS CODE
painted in red
across the chest.

▫ ▫ ▫ ▫

Watching the crowd,
hearing the laughs,
the shouted comments,
the whispered hisses . . .
I feel like *I'm* the one
being pointed at,
laughed at,
humiliated,
over and over
in a boiling stew
of taunts
that trap.

Feet glued
to the spot,
you know you should run;

you *want* to run,
but something about
everyone surrounding you
catches you,
holds you there,
like an invisible net
made of loud words
that wrap around
your legs
and mind,
holding tight.

⌐ ⫠ ⫠ ▪

It's a terrible feeling
to be surrounded
by a crowd
and to know that
even with
so many people there,
you're actually
completely
alone.

▫ ▫ ▫ ▫

No way,
no how,
will I let the beige blob
have an Ace feast
for breakfast
today.

□ □ □ □

I grab Ace's elbow,
huffing under my breath,
Part of being a We
is not letting anyone
eat any *of you*
for any *meal*
ever
at
all.

Ace gulps,
Huh?
as we push our way
through the blob.
You think we're a We?

We cut through the blob,
careening past the laughs,
make it down the hall

where we hide for just a second
while the bell beeps its ring
and the blob dissolves.

We duck into room 113,
and even though it's just a stairwell now,
even though it's crammed full
of desks and broken chairs,
it still *almost* feels like the safe space
from last summer,
when we learned that being divergent
was a thing to be proud of,
not a thing to hide.

I drag Ace all the way to the space
way back under the stairs,
dark, hidden from sight,
where we have to bend our necks
to see each other's eyes.

Ace looks off-balance,
almost scared,
no sparkle,
no glam,
no smirk,
no gold,
just a stunned face
I barely recognize.

Ace swallows,
and the words
scatter out,
like gravel
dumped from a shoe:

Th-thank you.
This was . . .
unexpected.
I mean . . .
Mr. Mann said
if I got one more DRESS CODE,
the consequences would be DIRE,
but I just thought
extra detention,
not this. . . .

Ace looks down at the poncho.
A sticky stain drips down
between the word *DRESS*
and the word *CODE,*
and there are other
unidentified
blotches, too. . . .
Maybe mold?
Grosssss.

Ace's face twists,
dissolving
into the blackest hole
of frowns.

Mr. Mann grabbed me,
like actually grabbed my arm,
and dragged me,
like actually dragged me,
into the front office
and said I had to wear this
or . . .
or . . . he'd call my grandma.
And Ben Y,
that is NOT a thing
that can happen.
I had no idea
they could DO this
to someone.
Did you?

Ace takes a breath
that's also
a bit of a hiccup.

Hey,
I say,
That jerd can eat my farts.
No, he can eat OUR farts.
Our *farts.*
Because we're a We.

Ace's head tilts to the side
just a smidge more
to see me better
I guess
in the shadows
under the stairs.

A tiny tiny half smile
sneaks into the corner
of Ace's mouth.

Are you wearing a belt under that thing?

Ace nods.

Excellent.
I have an idea.
Hand it over.

□ □ □ □

Okay. Yes.
I can own this look.
Ace laughs,
looking down
at our belts crisscrossed
over the words *DRESS CODE*
in a Conan the Barbarian
kind of way.

Then,
out of nowhere,
Ace hugs me tight
and whispers,
Thank you.

Over Ace's shoulder,
I see Jordan on the stairs,
looking down,
twirling a bathroom pass.

Jordan starts to wave,
but brushes his bangs
from his face instead
and then walks back
the way he came.

Ace lets go quickly,
saying,
Sorry.
I probably should have asked first.
Before the hugging.
Not everyone likes that.

It's okay,
I say.
But my mind is on Jordan now,
and why he didn't say hi.

Jordan never
doesn't say hi.

◻ ◻ ◻ ◻

For a second
we both stand there,
under the stairs,
saying nothing,
lost in our own worlds.

I snap back to now,
nod once,
put my hands on my hips,
and do my best
Ms. J impression:

Looking good, Ace.
Now go to class.
Own it.
Flaunt it.
Make it work.

Ace grins,
runs back into the main hallway,
and disappears
with a see-it-from-space
poncho swoosh
(that reminds me
just a little bit
of Ms. J's
swooshy caftans).

When I'm five seconds
from class,
I take a corner too fast,
and I smash into
a glob of girls
outside the bathroom.

Hey, it's *Ben Who What Why*!
someone says.

Hey, you're right,
IT is Ben Who What Why!
someone else says with a sniff
like the word *IT* has a smell
no one likes.

Hey, how's IT going, Ben Who What Why?
The first voice asks,
like I would actually answer.

Fire crawls,
crackling up my face,
sizzling my eyes
as I try
to push by
the glob.

Ben Who What Whyyyyy are you so rude?
Can't you hear us talking to you?

▫ ▫ ▫ ▫

The edges
of my vision
go dark,
a closing circle
of rage
as I turn,

delivering
one
gentle
dead-leg bonk
to the back
of Annabelle's knee,
tumbling her
to the ground,
so I can easily
twist her around
to look up at me,
squeezing her lips
between my fingers
like I've grabbed a fish
and am about
to pry out
a wriggling mess
of words
or worms
from
ITS
mouth.

Oh, am I rude?
Sorry *about that!*

My words smile at her surprise,
while she squeals through her nose,
while her friends squeal at her side,
and my pinpoint
refocuses.

How now
to cram my sincere
and heartfelt
apologies
via my fist
down Annabelle's
vibrating,
car-alarming
throat?

□ □ □ □

Miss Ybarra.
Get lost on your way to class?

Mr. Mann
appears
out of nowhere,
arms crossed,
voice loud:

RELEASE Miss Smith.
[very short pause]
Immediately.

I give Annabelle's mouth
one
last
twist
before I let go,
with maybe
possibly
a bit of a shove
away from me
for emphasis,
releasing her
back into the beige sea.

You can call me Mx. Ybarra.

The sparks fly from my mouth.
Their heat burns my eyes.

It's spelled M-x.
And it's used for anyone:
boys, girls, everyones.

Mr. Mann sighs deeply,
and uh-oh.
Mr. Mann's deep sighs
only mean one thing:
A speech is coming,
and it cannot be stopped.

MX. *Ybarra,*
I know this is a NEW concept,
BUT . . .
listen CAREFULLY.

Mr. Mann likes to
EMPHASIZE
certain WORDS
during
his SPEECHES
so that YOU
feel extra
DUMB.

He points his pointy nose
right at me
while he sniffs loudly
and barks out:

We are ALL
on a JOURNEY
TOGETHER
to Planet SAFE Space.
KINDNESS
is our fuel,
and without
KINDNESS FUEL . . .

He shrugs
like he can't help
what's about to happen,

YOU,
MX. Ybarra,
will be
LEFT BEHIND.

His chest puffs out
and he nods sharply
like that explains that.

I wipe Annabelle's lip gloss
off my fingers
and onto the concrete wall.

My eyes start to water.
Probably from all the burning
in my face.

I look at the smirks,
I hear the laugh-snorts
disguised as short coughs,
in the blob of beige.

I imagine a whole planet
made of Annabelles.

Fine by me!

My voice is louder than I expected.

PLEASE leave me behind!
I mean . . .
who wants to live on a planet
filled with mean boring monsters?
I choose
to blast off,
to literally
any
other
planet,
thanks.

I channel a smidge of Ace
as I face the blob,
stick out my tongue,
and give a small bow
before I turn and run.

□ □ □ □

But where am I running?
To gym?
No way.
I'm already gonna be soooo late
and I just cannot EVEN
with that hot mess today.

So I keep running.
Not to gym.
Not to room 113.
But out.
Out.
Out the school doors.
Down the sidewalk.
All the way to the bus stop
where I stop,
even though

I feel like
I could keep running
for days.

▫ ▫ ▫ ▫

Humid heat
melts the last
of the school AC
off my skin
as I breathe deep,
and decide
to keep running after all,
(to the next bus stop
at least)
so I can keep
smashing my feet
harder and faster
in front of me,
and I can keep
enjoying the feeling
of the seeping beige
melting off me,
in what I imagine
looks like
streaming steam,
billowing and huge,

being dissolved
and swallowed
by the deep blue sky
above me.

◦ ◦ ◦ ◦

The 315 pulls up
and I hold back
for just a second,
because this is
something
I never do,
like, ever.

Despite taking a vacation
from gym
every now and then,
I'm *really* not
a class-skipping
kind of kid.

But here I am
not only skipping class,
but about to skip
the whole rest of the day
of school?

That's like,
big-time trouble
if I get caught.

Except . . .
A thought explodes
in my brain,
opening my eyes
to the idea that . . .
honestly?
In-school suspension
would be kind of *nice*
if it meant no beige,
no hallways,
no comments my way
for a whole day
or week
or whatever
the punishment
would be.

▫ ▫ ▫ ▫

I fling myself
up the stairs
and onto the bus,
and I do the scan I always do.

But this time,
none of the faces on the bus
belong to the regulars I see
in the mornings.
There are none of the smiles or nods
I'm used to getting
in the afternoons.

That makes me feel extra alone,
and it's a little scary, actually,
like I took the wrong bus,
or like the world becomes
a different place
during the day
when I'm in school.

At my stop,
I leap off,
keep running,
and thank goodness
my house is still there,

not different
or weird
or gone.
Not that I
really thought
it would be,
but I'm relieved
just the same.

▫ ▫ ▫ ▫

I put in the garage code,
throw my hip into the door,
burst into the kitchen,
and wow.

I haven't been at home
in the middle of the morning
in the middle of the week
since,
I don't know,
maybe ever?

I guess I really am,
technically,
a class-skipping,

school-skipping
kind of kid
now.

Is that a benefit,
or a side effect
of my new look?

▫ ▫ ▫ ▫

I go to Benicio's room,
leap on his bed,
thinking maybe
possibly
I could take a nap,
even though,
weirdly,
his pillow is missing,
but then—
wait—
what was that noise?
There it is again . . .
like a cat's howl,
but quieter,
more sad,
stretched-out,
and close by,

like,
right here,
in the house,
coming from
just down the hall.

□ □ □ □

Mom's bedroom door
isn't closed all the way
for maybe the first time
in the history
of ever,
and I can tell
from the shiver down my neck,
and the rising hairs on my arms
that the
stretched-out
quiet
sad
howl
is coming
from inside.

□ □ □ □

Of course I think,
AHHH GHOST
because that's
the first thing
anyone would think
when they hear
a stretched-out
quiet
sad
howl
coming from
a barely open door
at the end of the hall.

(Even if it's the door
to their mom's bedroom,
and even if,
previously,
there have been no ghosts
heard
or seen
in the house.)

But as I get closer—

(Why, feet?
Why would you think
it's okay
to bring me closer
to the sound
instead of away???)

As I get closer—
the sound slides
into my brain
and chisels away
at a memory
buried deep.

I know this sound.
It's not a ghost.
It's Mom.
Crying.
On her knees.
Overcome with grief.
Just like that day
that feels like yesterday
but also a million years ago,
Benicio's funeral,
where we all made sounds
like animals

because none of us
knew how to be a human
in a world
without him.

◦ ◡ ◡ ◦

I peek through the crack,
where the door
isn't quite shut,
and watch Mom,
kneeling by her bed,
like she's praying,
but instead,
her face is buried
in Benicio's pillow,
muffling her howls,
but not hiding
her grief at all,
and I back away,
the hairs on my arms
still standing,
the back of my neck
still tingling,
because this is—

worse?
scarier?
more surprising?—
than finding
a real live ghost
in the house.

Mom doesn't cry.
Not anymore.

Mom is tired, sure.
Mom gets lost in her thoughts, sure.
Mom prays for our souls, sure.
And, sometimes,
on good days,
Mom makes bad jokes.
Sure.
But she never cries.
Not anymore.

At least,
that's what I thought.
That's how it seemed,
day after day
after day
after day.

But this?
This means what?
Does she come home from work
to howl before lunch?
Does she do it a lot?

I back my way
back down the hall
back through the kitchen
back to the garage
back outside
back to the bus stop
back to the 315
and back to school
where everything
might be awful,
but at least it isn't
cat-howl terrifying
in the middle of the morning.

BACK AT SCHOOL

The library
at Hart Middle School,
Home of the Rockets,
always has a low rumble
made of laughing
and chatting
and kids making stuff
or working on puzzles,
or even studying.

Before school,
during school,
after school,
it's like the brain
or maybe the heart
of the building,
sucking in
and pumping out
laughs and thoughts,
nonstop.

As soon as I escape
from whatever
just happened
at home,
(and after realizing
my backpack
is still taking a nap
on Benicio's bed
without me,
totally ruling out
going to the last
fascinating half
of Earth Science),
I let the brain
or the heart
or whatever the library is
suck me in
so I can find my own
quiet, private place
to take a big deep breath
and maybe another one
after that.

□ □ □ □

I lie on the floor
between the shelves
in the wayback stacks
hiding from all the everythings
this day is throwing at me,
and also to hide from Ms. J,
who would ask me
a zillion questions
if she saw me,
and who would
look *Concerned*
in that way she does
that makes me want to cry
and also punch things.

So, yeah.
I'm hiding.
On the floor.
Staring up
at the water stain
on the ceiling
and not knowing
what to think
about
what I just saw at home.

□ □ □ □

As I lie there,
on the scratchy floor,
breathing in the smells
of books I'll never read,
listening to the murmurs
of kids who aren't my friends,
and the cackles of Ms. J
bossing everyone around,
my shoulders finally relax
and my breathing calms down,
and it strikes me,
like a lightning bolt
to my lightning-rod head,
that this floor,
right here
in this library,
right here
in this reference section,
right here
where five-paragraph essays go to die . . .
THIS is the place
where un-beige,
baldy Ben Y
actually feels . . .

safe.

Like, *safe* safe.
Like, really safe.
Like, deep-breaths safe.
Like, Benicio-hug safe.

The *library.*
Huh.

□ □ □ □

Oh my tiny baby cheeses, Ace!
What in the WORLD?

After I hear Ms. J's shout,
I jam my head
between dictionaries,
hopefully staying hidden,
while I peek out
just a bit.

She's holding a stapler
next to a gigantic poster
that is almost as hideous
as Ace's poncho.

The poster is giant.
There are stars.
There are two big planets,
one on one side of the giant poster,
one on the other.

In the middle it says:

Hart Middle School Rockets
Blasting off together
to Planet Safe Space!

There's also a LOT of rockets.
The rockets are . . . parked (?) on one big planet.
One big planet is empty
and alone.

Smaller words
over the rocket parking-lot planet say:

Fuel up with kindness
and rocket your way
to Planet Safe Space!

Even smaller words under that say:

Every student will put their name on a rocket. For each observed kindness a student performs, the student's rocket will move closer to Planet Safe Space. This is a zero-tolerance anti-bullying initiative created to end bullying as we know it while rewarding acts of kindness. Participation is mandatory.

Ms. J rubs her temples,
like my mom does
after a long day.

Who made you wear that, Ace?

Ace tries to smile.
It's pretty wobbly.
Maybe only 40-watt.

*I'll give you three guesses
and the first two
don't count.*

Ms. J nods,
looking like
she might
want to cry
or explode
or both.

*Go take it off, Ace.
Right now.
Leave it in my office.
Then get to class.
And if Mr. Mann says
one word to you about it,
tell him to come find me.*

Ace runs to her office,
and when Ms. J thinks
no one is looking,
she snaps the stapler
four times
like an angry alligator
while muttering:

Safe space, my butt.

▫ ▫ ▫ ▫

After a while,
the bell beeps its ring
and I make a break for it,
trying to get
to the bathroom
before the crowds,
and also trying to disappear
for a minute or two,
so I can walk *back*
into the library
as if I had not just been there
for a long time,
lying on the floor.

This was my plan, anyway,
until I hear a voice behind me,
shouting:

Ben Y?
Where did you come from?
Where are you going?
Don't forget Newspaper Typing Club!

□ □ □ □

So, yeah.
I go to the bathroom.
And then go back to the library.
But this time
I sit in a chair
instead of
hiding on the floor.

□ □ □ □

In that short time
Ben B appeared
and Ms. J disappeared
and there are loud rumbles
coming from behind
the closed door
of Ms. J's office.

What's going on over there?
I toss myself into a seat
next to Ben B,
who's typing something
faster
than I've ever seen
anyone type anything
ever.

Ben B keeps typing,
says,
Where? Ms. J's office?
and how in the world
can he type
and talk
about different things
at the same time?

GAH. Ben Y!
You made me type office!

Ha! He can't!
Jordan flops down,
on the other side of Ben B,
looks to see
where I'm looking,
and says:

What's going on over there?

That's what I just said,
I say.

There's a slam.
We all look over.
Mr. Mann storms
past us,
backs up,
looks at me,
yells:

Cut-off shorts!
DRESS CODE!
and tosses a detention slip
that flutters to the ground
like an exhausted moth.

What?
Why?
It's after school!
Come on!

He storms off,
nearly crashing into Javier.

No hoodies in school!
DRESS CODE!

He throws a detention slip
at Javi,
whose arms fly up like,

What?
Why?
It's after school!
Come on!

Then Ace appears,
as if on cue,
rushing into the library
as Mr. Mann rushes out,
and Mr. Mann yells,
WAY too loud
for a library setting:

DON'T THINK YOU WON TODAY, SPORT.
DISTRICT POLICY ALWAYS WINS.
DRESS CODE!
He tosses a yellow slip
that lands at Ace's feet.
And disappears
out the door.

What's going ON over here?
Ms. J swoops over,
appearing from nowhere,
eyes in five places at once.

What was going on over there?
My face points to Ms. J's office,
and my accidentally
(but maybe not *that* accidentally)
bossy tone demands
that Ms. J's many eyes
swivel to me all at once.

Ace shuffles up,
just after Javi,
slumping into the seat
next to me.

Cheers.
Ace holds up the detention slip.
I knock mine into it.
Cheers.

Javi cheerses his
from across the table,
hoodie still on,
and now
with only his nose
poking out.

Done!
Ben B yanks his hands
from his keyboard,
crosses his arms,
leans back in his chair,
and looks at all of us
like a dog that just finished a bone.

After a second
his face morphs into
the one a kid makes
as he realizes
he just shouted a thing
while other people
were talking.

▫ ▫ ▫ ▫

You first.
Ms. J crosses her arms,
glances out the window
at the empty hallway,
glances back at Ben B,
who sits up straighter
and flashes a smile.

It's all done.

When no one says anything,
Ben B huffs,
"Using Sandbox Skills to Make Real Life More Awesome."
My article.
For the newspaper.
That was due today.
Don't we all have articles due today?

Not me!
Ace's smile
is not quite as
fresh-mint sparkly
as usual.
Today is my very first day
of newspapering.

Jordan sighs deeply.

Newspapering *is* our *word.*

I don't know if anyone
other than me
can hear
the soft mumbles
he aims at his shoes.

Just like you y'alls *is our thing, and meeting under the stairs is*
our *thing, and . . .*

He trails off,
swinging his feet
and scuffing his heels
into the scratchy old carpet.

I'm surprised
spidery lightning
doesn't shoot out
from Ms. J's eyes
and nose
and mouth
when she says:

I'm sorry, Ben B.
It appears your time has been wasted.

She clenches her jaw,
and I look for
angry sparks
flashing between
her grinding teeth.

Her low voice
thunders,
I have just learned
Mr. Mann
is demanding
oversight
of the entire newspaper.
Or else he's shutting it down.

Her giant hoop earrings quiver
as she watches her words
settle into our ears.

Wh-what does overs-sight *m-mean?*

Javier asks the question for all of us,
and if Javier is worried enough
to say something out loud,
before anyone else,

well,
that makes my stomach twist
into about ten extra knots.

◻ ◻ ◻ ⌐

All eyes
are on Ms. J
as we all seem to
swallow back
a burpy feeling
of *Yikes* and *Uh-oh*
and *What's going on*
all rolled up
in one.

He claims administration
needs to preauthorize
all newspaper topics,
per new rules
about ensuring
all student-created content
fits Planet Safe Space
anti-bullying criteria.

Jordan's confused *HUH??*
speaks for all of us.

Ms. J unrolls the papers
I didn't notice
she was crushing,
and she holds up
a page
with a typed list.

These are the authorized topics.

AUTHORIZED TOPICS FOR THE HART TIMES

Hart Middle Voted Best School in District

Hart Middle Offers Most Competitive Academics

Hart Middle Educators Embrace Assessment Curriculum

Hart Middle Sports Lead the District in Excellence

Admin Profile about Safe Space Initiative (See Mr. Mann

for details)

Can't wait to see you guys make the Hart Times great again!

So . . .
I have to start all over again?
On something new?
But I just finished!

Ben B sinks his head
into his hands
like he just found out
someone added
six more hours
to every school day.

Wh-what even i-is th-this list?
Javier's nose crinkles
through the hole
he's pulled tight
in his hoodie.
Wh-what i-is P-p-p—

Planet Safe Space??

Javier whips around,
his scrunched nose
pointing at Jordan now.

Jordan should really
really
know better
than to finish Javi's sentences,
especially after last summer.

Sorry, Javier. Sorry. I got excited. Well, not excited in a good
way, excited in a confused and wondering way. And I didn't
know if maybe you missed the announcement even though
it didn't explain much and . . . never mind. I'm sorry. I didn't
mean to put words in your mouth. I know you hate that.

Jordan holds out his fist
for an apology fist bump
and after a second,
Javier knocks it with his elbow

We just invented a fistbow bump, Javi. Hahaha. Good job us.

◦ ◦ ◦ ◦

So we have to write about this stuff now?
Hurt Middle Voted Best School in District??
Is that even true?
How can we write about it if it isn't even true?

Ben B's bottom lip sticks out,
an impressive pout
probably perfected by years
of unfair moments,
and probably none of them
worse than right now.

Ms. J looks so droopy,
so sad,
so mad,
all at once,
I think maybe *she's* invented
a new emotion
all on her own.

Authorized topics only.
It's that, or no newspaper.
New rules are still rules.
My hands are tied, you y'alls.

Can't we just say thank you for your service to the newspaper
part of Newspaper Typing Club and just have Typing Club
again? None of us really liked the newspaper idea anyway.
No offense.

You forget, Jordan,
Ms. J sighs.

Adding the newspaper part
to Newspaper Typing Club
is what allowed us to keep *Typing Club*
in the first place.
Remember: no newspaper,
no substance,
and no substance
means no typing club.

Ben B sucks in his pout,
growling,

But Sandbox is MADE of substance!
It's, like, ONLY substance!

Ms. J holds up
her *Stop* hand.

I know, Ben B,
believe me.
And watch your tone.

Her *Stop* hand
turns to a pointing finger
at Ben B's
mad mouth.

Mr. Mann is my boss,
and . . .

She lays her head
on the table,
forehead down.

And whoa.
I don't want to see that.
Not today.
Not any day.
Ms. J never gives up.
And neither do I.
Neither do any of us.

▫ ▫ ▫ ▫

Give me that.
I make a grabby hand
for the list of topics,
and Ace throws a page at me,
folded like a paper airplane.

I look down at the list,
and watch the letters
swirl and jump
until their dance
(mostly) makes sense.

If we could survive summer school,
and read a whole
entire
book
out loud,
and retake the FART,
and teach this one—

I jab my thumb at Ms. J
and roll my eyes
in a jokey way

—to play Sandbox
like she's a pro,
then we can do this, right?
If working on
a boring
dumb mess
of a Mr. Mann—approved newspaper
means saving
all of our fun and awesome
Typing Club time with Ms. J—
then we have to do it, right?

Ben B stares at the table,
looks up,
sighs,
and says:

I mean,
she doesn't even know
how to spend all her gold yet,
and she's still really terrible
at killing pigs for pork chops,
and who knows
how the Sandbox library would turn out
without any of us here to help . . .
Okay. Fine.
Ms. J still really needs Typing Club.
Obviously.
And besides, if I quit Newspaper Typing Club,
my parents will freak.
I'll have to go back to language arts tutoring
TWO times a week.
And I hate tutoring
more than anything.

Jordan whispers:
Tutoring
as he makes a quiet fart noise
and gets shushed
by Ms. J,
who looks like
she might cry
after Ben B's speech.

Ben B sighs again.
I'll take:
Hart Middle Voted Best School in District.
I guess.

Jordan mumbles,
I would be so sad if I had to go home and play regular Sandbox
instead of Secret School Typing Club Sandbox so I guess I'll
take Hart Middle Offers Most Competitive Academics even
though I fell asleep saying that out loud.

Javier sticks his tongue out
like he just sucked on
a rotten lemon
and taps the page.
Th-this one:
Hart Middle Educators Embrace Assessment Curriculum.

Ace says,
I'll take the one about Hart Middle Sports Blah Blah.
Because I am so sporty.
Obviously.

I look at the list.
Only one authorized topic left.

Oh, come on, you y'alls!
You left the worst one for me!

Admin profile!
Do I have to interview Mr. Mann?!

Jordan punches my shoulder.
Thanks for taking one for the team, Ben Y, you are a true hero.

Ben B holds up two fingers
and nods solemnly at me.

Javier holds up
a quick sketch
of a trophy
that says:

Ben Y
MVP
(of Newspapering)

Ace offers a high five.

Ben Y is showing off
alllll the hero moves today!

I weakly slap Ace's hand,
then slump back in my seat.

Great.

▫ ▫ ▫ ▫

The glow
that grows
on Ms. J's face
is so warm
and big,
it makes me
look away
because it feels
private somehow
(even though
we're all
staring at her
across the table).

□ □ □ □

Ben Y.

She puts her hand on her chest,
takes a deep breath,
like she's steadying herself
before diving into
the deep end.

Thank you for that.

I let my glance
catch hers
super fast
so I can say
just with my eyes
and my face
(but not my loud mouth
for once):
Okay, great,
awesome, cool,
don't make it weird.

▫ ▫ ▫ ▫

But she makes it weird
by running off,
her caftan
flowing behind her
like rippling
stingray
wings.

▫ ▫ ▫ ▫

In a flash she's back,
with an armload of . . .
what?

She dumps the pile of papers
all over our table,
breathless
as she says,
And there's more where THAT came from.

We look down.
It's a bunch of old *Hart Times*.
Like *really* old.

For inspiration,
she says,
and the tips of her ears
glow bright red.

Jordan grabs one,
looks it over,
looks up,
eyes wide.

*These are from nineteen eighty-eight?? Are they all about
dinosaurs?*

Ben B laughs,
I bet they're written *by dinosaurs.*

Ms. J makes a noise
kind of like
I imagine
a dinosaur might
before it chased you down
to eat you.

□ □ □ □

Ben B is the first to yell:

NO WAY!

Then Jordan cracks up
so hard and fast,
he falls from his chair
splat
on the floor.

Javier's deep chuckle
fills the air
and I finally recognize
the reporter photo,

blurry and faded,
appearing on nearly
every front page
in the pile.

No way.
Nuh-uh.

Ms. J!!
Is this YOU???

▫ ▫ ▫ ▫

All of our laughs
fold together,
crashing in on themselves
again and again,
endless waves
as we page through
stacks and stacks
of old newspapers
(and yearbooks!)
Ms. J pulls out of
the dusty shelves.

Her glasses were so giant,
magnifying her eyes,
making her look
constantly surprised
in every blurry photo
we can find.

Those were the STYLE,
Ms. J snorts,
wiping sparkling tears
from the corners
of her laughing eyes.
The coolest of the cool.

That makes us laugh even harder.

▫ ▫ ▫ ▫

So, wait . . .

Ace taps a *Hart Times*
on the top of a stack.

Your name is also
Jordan Jackson?

Jordan shouts:
No relation! And how did you know my last name, Ace? You
ARE a detective, aren't you?

Ace grins at Jordan
like Jordan is five
and said something
dumb but cute.

Your name is everywhere, dude.
Backpack.
Lunch box.
Your shoes.
Doesn't take a detective
to see it. . . .
It's kinda hard to miss.

Well *I* hadn't really noticed before,
but, yeah,
Jordan does write
JORDAN JACKSON
in different patterns
and designs
all over . . .
everything.

Jordan's face scrunches
while Ace's sandpaper laugh
whisper-scratches
back and forth.

My face scrunches, too.
I don't like Ace's tone
toward Jordan.
It's super not cool.

▫ ▫ ▫ ▫

Ben B interrupts
the suddenly
uncomfortable
moment.

Did you write the whole newspaper, Ms. J?
All by yourself?
Why didn't you tell us until now?

Ben B holds up a holiday edition.
A headline shouts:
"THE BIGGER THE HAIR, THE BIGGER YOU SHINE"

No.
Not the whole paper.
But . . .
there was a . . .
let's say . . .
revolving staff.
I might have been a little too . . .
editorial . . .
here and there.

Ms. J shakes her head,
takes the paper from Ben B,
flips through it, smiles.

I had a lot of ideas
about a lot of things
and was never wrong
about anything
Just like every middle schooler,
amiright?

Ben B, Jordan, Javier, and I
all groan long and loud,
at exactly the same time,
and our voices

link together
one at a time
stringing together the words:
Ms. J, please.
Never say
amiright
ever again.

□ □ □ □

Yeah!
Don't be such a . . .
grown-up!

Ace joins in,
interrupting,
not quite understanding
the way
the rest of us
know how
to tease Ms. J
in just the right way
to almost get in trouble,
but not.

□ □ □ □

I can't believe
I almost forgot
Ace was even here.

And based on
the awkward silence
and the awkward looks
and Ace's awkward words
still hanging
in the air
above us all,
it kind of looks like
maybe Ace wishes
not to be here
anymore.

▫ ▫ ▫ ▫

I flip though
paper after paper
and notice –

Ha!

She had a regular feature:
"Jordan's Hot Takes!"

When I start laughing,
I don't think I can stop.
Not many things
are worth reading,
at least not to me
when I have to
chase down the letters,
flip them around,
solve new puzzles,
over and over,
until I forget
what the story was
to begin with. . . .

But this?
This is worth it.

"Jordan's Hot Takes"?????

Ms. J pinches her nose
right at the bridge,
like she might be regretting
this source
of inspiration.

*Just some thoughts
about pop culture.
That's all.*

That's all??
She *blisters* movie stars
and musicians
and a bunch of people
I've never heard of,
but who must be famous,
because no way
would anyone ever
ever
allow a kid to say these things
about other kids.

She goes after their clothes,
she goes after their acting,
their song lyrics,
their hairstyles.

It's so funny.
It's so mean.

It's giving me
a LOT
of inspiration.

HOME

I don't think you should be in here.
Benicio would hate it.
Are those my markers?
You should ask before you use my stuff.
And you can't even ask Benicio,
so you probably shouldn't use his stuff
ever
at all.

Esme's chirps
twist and bend
behind me,
accusing,
alarmed,
almost . . .
hurt-sounding.

I turn around,
Benicio's chair
squealing in protest.

You're right, Esme Esme bo-besme.
Can I use your markers?

Esme hugs the doorway,
quiet for a second,
before whisper-chirping:

I don't think so.
I want them back.
Right now.

She holds out her hand,
but doesn't walk through the door.

Also, you have a desk in our room.
You should find your own markers and sit there.
Also also, Mom said to tell you dinner is ready.

She hangs on to the doorframe
for a few more seconds,
making a grabby hand at me.

I hold up the markers.

If you want them,
come get them,
Esme Esme bo-besme.
Benicio's ghost won't eat you.

Esme flings herself back,
like the doorway is suddenly
on fire.

She squeaks down the hall,
yelling:

Mo-om!!!
Benny took my markers!!!

I spin the chair
to face my mess again.

I know that was mean . . .
to say the thing
about Benicio's ghost.

But I'm almost done.
And I don't want
to work at the desk
in our room.
I want to sit here.
At this desk.
Benicio's desk.
For inspiration.

Esme can have her markers back
in, like, five minutes.

◻ ◻ ◻ ◻

For a second I think maybe . . .
maybe . . .
I should call a meeting
before school
in room 113
under the stairs
so I can show this to Jordan.
And Ben B.
And Javier.
What if they want to help?
What if they can make it even better?

But also . . .
it's so much easier
to do it myself,
to finish tonight,
to not argue about anything,
to make my own choices
about what to say
or what to draw.

It feels really nice,
actually,
to just do my own thing

with no rules
and with no one
to boss
or be bossed.

□ □ □ □

Mom yells,
DINNER, BENNY!
like it's a
red-alert
category-five
emergency
instead of just . . .
dinner.

I sweep everything off the desk
and into a drawer
to hide it
until I get back,
and I run down the hall
before Mom screams
any more.

□ □ □ □

What's going on?
With you?
These days?

Mom rolls her words
around the spaghetti
in her mouth
before saying:

Sorry.
Should have waited
until my mouth wasn't full.

Esme says,
Well, she's stealing my markers,
she's sneaking into Benicio's room,
she's . . .
her chirps become
background sounds,
just like
the little baby birds
outside.

I stop twirling my noodles,
think about Mom's question,
because there are

so
many
things
going
on. . . .

Bald head.
Newspaper Typing Club.
The beige blob.
That jerd, Mr. Mann.
Ace and . . . Ace things.
Skipping class too much.
Skipping school that one time.
Seeing Mom crying.
And and and and—
and maybe *I*
should be asking *Mom*
what's up with HER these days,
except I don't want to ask,
because I'm afraid
of what sad feelings
that might jiggle loose,
and and and—

By the look on your
beautiful
but stunned face,

my guess is:
Nothing, Mom.
Everything is great.

Mom imitates me,
and her voice sounds like mine,
but twisted down,
like Eeyore's ears
in voice form.

She puts her hand on mine,
looks up from her plate,
says in an Eeyore voice,
Even when everything is not great,
remember, You Are Loved.

Mom makes me wonder
more times than not
what she actually means
when she tells me,
You Are Loved.
Right now, it feels more like:
You Are a Joke.
Or worse,
it feels like
she's just saying words

that are sounds
to fill up the air
before the quiet
can swallow us
whole.

□ □ □ □

Esme's voice
squeaks
around the edges
of my conversation
with Mom.

Is anyone even listening *to me?*
Does anyone
want to know
about anything
going on with me?

I drop my fork,
stand,
take my plate,
smash it into the sink,
walk away.

What??
Mom calls after me.
I'm serious, mija.
You are loved!
I want to make sure you're doing okay.
I really do want to know . . .
what is going on with you?
For real.

Nothing, Mom!
I Am Loved!
That solves everything, right?
Right!
So, yeah. Fine.
I'm always great,
just like you're always great!
Everything is the greatest great
that ever greated.
Happy now?

I yell the words
as I march down the hall
slam the door
and hurl myself
back into
Benicio's chair.

▫ ▫ ▫ ▫

I like it in his room.
It's quiet in here.

And it's the only place
free free free
of Mom's questions
and Esme's chirps.

I think . . .
I hope . . .
Benicio's ghost
won't eat me.

I think . . .
I hope . . .
Benicio's ghost
would understand.

BEFORE

0BenwhY: sometimes I would like to stuff mom in a T-shirt launcher like those ones at basketball games

0BenwhY: and I would like to blast her into orbit

0BenwhY: could you make a potion for that?

0BenwhY: T-shirt launcher rocket fuel

0BenwhY: for sending moms to moons?

SB10BEN: well, hello to you, too.

SB10BEN: I'm doing well today, thanks for asking.

SB10BEN: oh, what was that? you just noticed the whole cage of milked fairies? yes. YOU'RE WELCOME.

0BenwhY: 😖

0BenwhY: HOW

0BenwhY: ARE

0BenwhY: YOU

0BenwhY: DOING

0BenwhY: TODAY

0BenwhY: GREAT?

0BenwhY: GREAT

SB10BEN: You know, sometimes it's nice to pretend you're interested in other people

SB10BEN: before you launch into complaining and complaining and complaining

OBenwhY: omg, Benicio!

OBenwhY: I'm going to launch you to the moon, too!

SB10BEN: What's going on, grasshopper? Why are you so annoying, I mean *annoyed*?

OBenwhY: nothing.

SB10BEN: oh come on. you can't come in here, T-shirt cannons blazing, and then say *nothing*.

OBenwhY: it's . . . whatever.

OBenwhY: mom is mom

OBenwhY: she just doesn't listen.

OBenwhY: i was very nice and polite and i even washed the dishes

OBenwhY: without being asked!

OBenwhY: and mom was like, ooooh, shhhh, Esme, don't tell Benita she has the day wrong

OBenwhY: ooooh, esme, don't tell Benita it's not my birthday for two months

OBenwhY: oooh, Esme, what do you think she wants? A surfboard? A pony?

OBenwhY: like, what? why is she making jokes when i'm doing something nice?

OBenwhY: I mean sometimes maybe I just do nice things, ok?

OBenwhY: what if I don't *have* a reason? or care what day it is?

OBenwhY why is it a joke if i'm being nice?

SB1OBEN: well

SB1OBEN: what DID you want?

SB1OBEN: what were you buttering mom up for?

OBenwhY: GAH. BENICIO! GIVE ME SOME CREDIT!

SB1OBEN:

OBenwhY: Fine. I wanted her to let me move into your old room.

OBenwhY: but she said no

SB1OBEN: What? Hahaha. Of course you can't have my room.

SB1OBEN: It's *my* bedroom, Benita!

OBenwhY: You moved a million miles away. You're a dumb grown-up now.

OBenwhY: You don't need an apartment there and a bedroom here.

SB10BEN: Why not?

SB10BEN: What if something happens here? What if I lose my job and have to move home?

OBenwhY: You can't lose your job! It's your company!

SB10BEN: I *started* the company, but now we have investors, earning reports to meet . . .

SB10BEN: I could TOTALLY lose my job and have to move home.

SB10BEN: I'm on Mom's side here. So. Still my room. For now.

SB10BEN: Plus, it has all my stuff in it.

OBenwhY: OLD stuff.

OBenwhY: Stuff you didn't need enough to bring with you.

OBenwhY: I knew you'd be on her side. you're always on her side. no one is ever on my side

SB10BEN: hey! I'm always on your side.

SB10BEN: Except for this one time.

OBenwhY: I hate mom.

OBenwhY: For real.

SB10BEN: Come on. Don't say that. What if she heard you say that?

SB10BEN: Mom is strong and fierce, just like you.

OBenwhY: I'm not YELLING it, dummy.

OBenwhY: This is a super private chat/server-within-a-server thing, right?

OBenwhY: if it's a private safe place for testing out super secret sandbox inventions, then I can say mean things without getting in trouble

OBenwhY: unless you're going to tell on me

OBenwhY: like a baby who still lives at home

SB10BEN: 😧

OBenwhY: 🔪 💀 ✏️

SB10BEN: Nothing is private, you know. Ever.

SB10BEN: If it's online, it's hackable, crackable, screenshot-able, whatever.

SB10BEN: Encrypted, even deleted, doesn't matter.

SB10BEN: If you put something online, you have to understand that it's basically floating in space.

SB10BEN: Anyone who's smart or determined enough to find it will find it.

SB10BEN: And they can do whatever they want with it. Projected into the sky? Cool. For everyone on Earth to see? Done.

SB10BEN: If you don't want it projected into the sky with your name and face attached, don't put it online.

SB10BEN: Remember that, okay?

OBenwhY: you're such a hippocrit, Benicio. THIS SECRET CABIN IS ONLINE 🙄

OBenwhY: I want your room

SB1OBEN: Not yet, grasshopper.

SB1OBEN: But maybe one day. If Sandbox is a hit and I'm a millionaire and it doesn't matter if I lose my job. 😊

OBenwhY: a MILLIONAIRE? Dream big, Benicio! 😁

SB1OBEN: Seriously. You never know.

SB1OBEN: and remember you don't hate mom. you're just mad. Mad is different than hate.

OBenwhY: mad is different than hate? hmm.

SB1OBEN: for real. think about that for a minute.

SB1OBEN: now, can we move along from this delightful conversation?

SB1OBEN: i was looking forward to testing new potions and building something with starstone

SB1OBEN: not arguing with you for my entire dinner break

OBenwhY: Starstone?! After all this time, you figured it out?!

SB1OBEN: Thanks to you . . . your idea about adding helium was spot-on. 🙌

OBenwhY: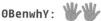

SB10BEN: Seriously. You're one of the smartest girls I know.

OBenwhY: Girls?

SB10BEN: Hate to break it to you, but even a super smart middle schooler like you is still a girl and not a grown-up.

OBenwhY: I know that! Just . . . can't I be the smartest KID you know? Or person?

SB10BEN: Um, sure. Definitely one of the top five ladypeoples.

OBenwhY: 😣 PEOPLEpeoples

SB10BEN: Fine. You drive a hard bargain.
SB10BEN: You are one of the top three smartest people peoples I've ever known.
SB10BEN: Better?

OBenwhY: Better.

SB10BEN: Well, this has been really, really fun, but I have to get to yet another meeting.

OBenwhY: Can't I just *see* the starstone? For a second?

SB10BEN: My dinner break is over. Sorry, grasshopper.

OBenwhY: okay, well, I'm sorry, too. For wasting all our starstone-building time being mad.

SB10BEN: that's okay. we got to build YOU up, instead of a starship.

OBenwhY: shuuuuuuttttttt uuuuupppppppp

SB10BEN: love you, little ~~sister~~ peopleperson

OBenwhY: love you too, big ~~annoying~~ brother

NOW

0BenwhY: I'm sitting at your desk

0BenwhY: at your computer

0BenwhY: reading through the old archive

0BenwhY: to see if there's anything smart I can learn

0BenwhY: but nah

0BenwhY: we were so dumb

0BenwhY: . . .

0BenwhY: kidding

0BenwhY: YOU were never dumb

0BenwhY: and your advice from back then still helps

0BenwhY: sometimes

0BenwhY: when it's not bad advice

0BenwhY: which it is

0BenwhY: sometimes.

0BenwhY: ha

0BenwhY: . . .

0BenwhY: . . .

0BenwhY: remember when you told me:

0BenwhY: nothing online is ever anyonyymous anonomous anoynoumous

OBenwhY: HOWEVER YOU SPELL IT

OBenwhY: and how everything online lives forever?

OBenwhY: ?

OBenwhY: well, what if I do something anonimus anonomos anonymuos IRL?

OBenwhY: on real paper. not online. will it live forever, too? will i get figured out?

OBenwhY: I can't decide if i *want* to get figured out or not.

OBenwhY: that's kind of weird, isn't it?

OBenwhY: . . .

OBenwhY: you're no help at all.

OBenwhY: about a lot of things these days

SCHOOL

Who chooses
who decides
who is cool
and who is weird
and who is dumb
and who is smart
and who fits here
and who fits there
and what is right
and what is wrong?

Who told *you*
your answer is right
and mine is wrong?

How are *you* the one
who decides
if something is cool
or something is trash?

What if,
for once,
you don't tell *me*.

What if,
for once,

you

step

back?

□ □ □ □

What if,
for once,
you see what it's like
for someone else
to define you,
as if their opinion of you
is fact?

Wonder if you'll like that?

□ □ □ □

I kept asking myself
those questions
and more
as I stayed up
super late

and found all the paper
in the whole house
and printed copies
until the ink ran out.

Now I hitch my stuffed backpack
over my shoulder
in an extra-gentle way
so my pages
can wait
until I get to school
super early
(and sneak in the side door
with the lock
that doesn't latch)
before they explode out,
shouting their unauthorized truths
all over the school.

It's like I can feel the papers
shaking and buzzing,
ready to flutter on a breeze
made of everyone's gasps,
and like little seeds,
they will plant themselves
everywhere

and grow
and grow
and grow
until everyone
is asking,
Who did this?
Where did this come from?
What is going on?

◻ ◻ ◻ ◻

I am a ninja,
sliding through the air,
sneaking past molecules,
bending around light,
silent,
running as fast as I can,
willing myself
to be quick
and actually invisible
for once,
dodging hallway cameras,
and thanking Benicio's ghost
for helping out this once,
because
WHEW

every teacher
is in one room
for some before-school
meeting,
and no one is around
to bust
my super sweet
ninja moves.

▫ ▫ ▫ ▫

The pages flutter behind me,
my seeds caught in the wind
before the storm.

I fling them,
I Frisbee them,
I toss,
I sling,
I even stack—
on a table over there,
on a chair right here.

By the time I'm at the doors
that lead to the stairwell,
the empty halls
are filled with
whispery papers.

I am breathless
as I sit on my old desk,
pushed to the side
in room 113,
which isn't a room at all,
and I pull my knees
tight to my chest,
and I wait
for the first bell,
for the first signs of life
from the seeds I just planted.

▫ ▫ ▫ ▫

I wonder if this is how lightning feels
just after it strikes
but before the fire starts.

▫ ▫ ▫ ▫

Shrieks fill the halls.
And laughter, too.
And hoots.
And hollers.
And oooohs.

And someone says,
Whoever did this
is HILARIOUS,
and another kid says,
I WISH I was that funny.
And someone else says,
Who could it be?
(without emphasizing the IT
at all.)
And I feel my chin lift up
all on its own,
and my smile
grow and grow and grow,
because even though
they don't know
they're talking about me . . .
I know they are.

Somehow,
right now,
them *not* knowing
and me knowing
what they don't know
fills me up.

Like . . .
I've never felt this
complete
before.

▫ ▫ ▫ ▫

All day,
in every class,
in every hallway,
every conversation
I overhear
is a version
of the same:

Who is the mystery writer?
What will happen now?
Why can't we figure out who did it?

And I think about saying:
I've been here all along, you dummies.
You just never bothered to pay attention
to who I really am,
to who I can actually be
if you take off
your beige glasses
and really *see* me.

But instead,
I say nothing.

Maybe it's weird,
but I don't *want* them to know.
I don't *want* to give away my secret.

Let them wonder,
Let them ask
Who
What
Why
and let *them*
feel what it's like
to have no answers
for once.

□ □ □ □

It makes me smile,
(maybe bigger
than I thought
a smile could be)
to imagine

all these kids
who've called me
Ben Who What Why
(and so much worse)
for so long;
these kids who think
not blending in
is somehow wrong—
suddenly, they
want to know who I am?
They want to be
as funny as me?

I wonder what they'd say
if they knew
the hilarious
mystery kid . . .
the one
they suddenly wish
they could be . . .
was me?

▫ ▫ ▫ ▫

Of course,
it only takes
about one minute
before Mr. Mann
huffs and puffs
down all the halls
yelling things like:
WHAT is that!
and
WHO is responsible for this?
and
WHY are you loitering?
Get to CLASS!

▫ ▫ ▫ ▫

First period.
Second period.
Third.
Lunch.

And not one shriek,
not one laugh,
not one hoot,
not one holler,
not one ooooh

has started
or ended
with
Hey, Ben Who What Why,
blah blah blah blah blah . . .

And THAT has not happened
since . . . I can't remember.

▫ ▫ ▫ ▫

I'm invisible today,
like the wind
or a ghost.
No earbuds necessary
to try to hide
In plain sight
because
poof
I'm gone.

No one is looking
at me
or my clothes
or my bald head
or my anything.

Well,
they *are* looking at my words,
even though
they don't know
those words are mine.

So yeah,
I'm invisible.

But also?
I'm everywhere.

▫ ▫ ▫ ▫

I close my eyes,
reveling in my happiness,
like a lizard soaking up
the white-hot sun.

I fill myself up with it.
I bask in it.
I eat it for lunch.

▫ ▫ ▫ ▫

Even in the library,
even after school,
even from my friends,
the communal freak-out
continues.

Ben B waves a wrinkled paper
at all of us
as he bursts into Newspaper Typing Club,
eyes wide.

Did you see this?
Did you read it?
I read the whole page,
and I don't read the whole
of anything.

Well, you did read all of Save Ur Server, Save Urself: A Many
Choices Sandbox Adventure Book, *because we ALL read all of*
it this summer, remember?

Not the point, Jordan!
Ben Y? Did you see this?
Of course you did,
everyone did.

So who did it?
It had to be one of us.
And it wasn't me,
so . . .

Not me! I stayed up way too late last night watching last night's
episode of Fierce Across America *over and over and over so*
that I could learn how to do THIS!

Jordan flings himself to the floor
and flops back and forth
in a wormy kind of wiggle
until he knocks into a chair
and has to stop.

Javier drops his bag,
plops his butt
in a chair,
makes a quick sketch,
tosses it out on the table.

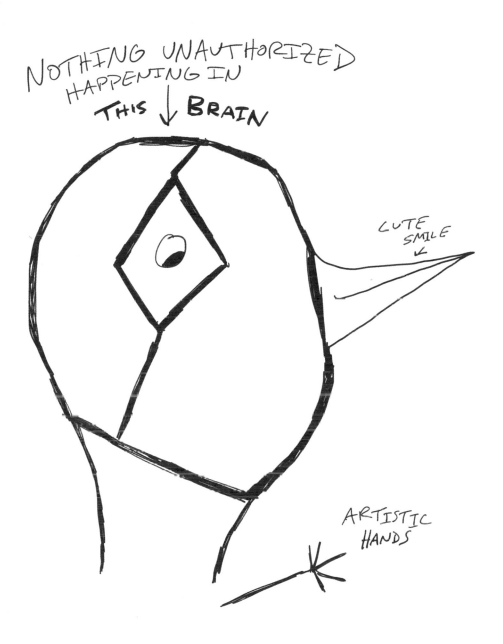

A door slams
and we all whip around
just in time
to see Mr. Mann storming
again
from Ms. J's office
like a very mad
cartoon sheriff.

He doesn't stop storming
as he shouts at all of us:

SOMEONE confesses
or EVERYONE is suspended!

And he disappears
out the door
without DRESS CODING
anyone
at all.

▫ ▫ ▫ ▫

A few minutes later,
Ms. J appears
with her trademark
caftan *swoooosh*
like she was a bat
a second ago
and has
boom
dropped out of the sky,
and I have to bite my lips,
like, really clamp down,
to keep from asking for
Jordan's Hot Take
on what's happening
in school today.

I don't have to ask, though,
because her hot take
steams like dragon breath
as she says,

Who did this?
WHO?

And, whoa,
she's WAY more mad
than I thought she'd be.
I thought she wanted to

inspire us
with the zings and burns
of her middle school words.

I thought she was secretly saying
we should all have a hot take
about all the unfair things
going on at Hart Middle.

But her dragon breath steams
as she hisses,

Well?
Who??

Everyone shouts,
Not me!
All at once.

My shout
is the loudest.

▫ ▫ ▫ ▫

I mean,
as much as I love it
that everyone
in the whole school

is hanging on
my every word,
I'm not ready
for anyone
to know
I'm the one
who did this.

I want to protect this secret
and feed it,
keeping it strong
and healthy,
so I can hold it tight
and visit it
at night,
when everything else
is the worst.

I want to write more
and say more
and get more
shrieks and laughs
and hoots and hollers
and oooohs
and even some gasps
the next time I do it.

I want to have more days
when no one sees me
or notices me
because they're too distracted
by the things I WANT them
to notice
and see.

I want to stretch this out,
hold it tight,
feel this power every day,
sleep soundly because of it
every night.

I want Ms. J
to calm down
and not be mad
and be *excited*
about all the
hot takes I have.

NO WAY I'm confessing.
NO WAY I'm giving in.

This is the best I've felt
in a hundred years.
(If I don't look at Ms. J.)

I'm ten feet tall right now.
(If I don't see the way
Ms. J's shoulders slump
in anger
and disappointment.)

□ □ □ □

Ace walks in
ten minutes late,
sees Ms. J quivering
over us
and pauses
before saying,

Hey, you y'alls.
What's up, Ms. J?

Ms. J holds up the paper,
shaking it at Ace.

Was this you?

And without even a pause,
Ace winks at me,
grins that 100-watt
fresh-mint grin,
and says,

Who else?

□ □ □ □

Wait.
WHAT.
IT WAS NOT!

□ □ □ □

I might have just
said that

Wait.
WHAT.
IT WAS NOT!

out loud.

□ □ □ □

omg
omg
omg

□ □ □ □

Everyone gasps.
Ms. J's mouth
becomes a very thin,
very straight,
very mad
line.

You two.
Follow me.
NOW.

□ □ □ □

We follow her
to her office,
which is, like,
some kind of
drama portal
these days.

Ace winks at me.
Again.
And I worry
for a second
about NOT getting suspended
and instead
going to jail
for strangling Ace
with Ace's own
wagging
blabbing
lying
tongue.

▫ ▫ ▫ ▫

Ms. J doesn't even sit.
I'm surprised
she doesn't take flight,
diving at our heads,
pecking at our eyes,
while she seethes:

We'll stay here all night.
Until one of you explains to me
WHAT is going on?
WHO thought this was a good idea?
WHY you would do this?

WELL??

▫ ▫ ▫ ▫

I look at Ace.
Ace looks at me.

I honestly
have no idea
what to say.

Why is Ace trying to steal this from me?
Except Ace doesn't know it was me.
Unless Ace *does* know it was me?
But how?

Calm down, self.
Think.
Think.

I mean, *anyone*
could be surprised enough
to shout WAIT WHAT IT WAS NOT!

Right?

Not just the one person
who is guilty
of doing the thing?

I cross my arms.
I narrow my eyes.
I clench my jaw.

I refuse to give up
the one thing
that's EVER
given me control over
where the beige blob looks
and what the beige blob thinks.

I won't let anyone take that from me.
Not Ace.
Not even Ms. J.

I'll stay here all night.
Easy.
I'm used to never sleeping.

###

When I showed you
those old Hart Times,
it wasn't to inspire you
to go rogue.
It was to inspire you
to pay attention.
To be creative.
To show you

how you can take any topic,
even authorized *ones,*
and make it yours.

But this . . .
this is super not okay.

It's almost like I can see the thoughts
skating behind her eyes—
clouds racing across
a stormy sky,
crashing together
into one
big
storm.

You need to listen to me carefully.

It's as if her mouth and eyes
and cheeks and forehead
all got assigned a different emotion
at the exact same time.
She chews her lips into a pucker.

This is a punishable offense.
A suspended from school,
on your permanent record,
really, really zero-tolerance type of offense.

My mouth goes dry.
Ace's army boots
shuffle back and forth,
back and forth.

Ms. J looks at me
for a really long time,
takes a long, deep breath,
rolls her shoulders back,
sits up straight.

You know what?
She exhales her words,
holds up a hand:
Don't tell me anything else.
I don't want to know.

From here on out,
I need to preserve
some *amount of*
plausible deniability.

▫ ▫ ▫ ▫

Ace glances at me
as if to ask the same thing
I'm thinking:

Plausi—
whowhat?

□ □ □ □

Ms. J continues,
her voice lower than before,
her eyes flashing.

I know nothing.
Except for this:
No more
unauthorized editions
of ANYTHING.
You hear me?

We watch her nod slowly,
as if that will make us nod, too.
What else can we do?
We nod, too.

I need some time . . .
to digest what you've done.

Ace whispers:
Even though
you know nothing
about it?

Ms. J hisses back:
Exactly.
Now go home.
Work on your authorized *articles.*

We both leap up,
run out,
before she changes her mind.

□ □ □ □

Now that I know
I'm getting out of the library alive,
I can plan exactly how
I will kick Ace in the butt,
so hard and so many times,
that the Man in the Moon
is renamed
the Ace in the Moon.

□ □ □ □

When we're far enough
from Ms. J's office
that she can't hear us,
probably,
Ace flips around,
facing me,

grinning bigger
and shinier
than ever.

Well??
You're welcome.

My mouth gapes,
surprise paralyzing
my words.

You want to know a secret?
I didn't even really know it was you.
Except that you're funny . . .
and you're into fashion . . .
and you hate Mr. Mann . . .
and since you and I are the only people I know
with those three awesome qualities . . .
it was an easy guess!

Ace bows,
stopping me
in my tracks.

I took the heat off of you,
blasted it on me.
Boom.
You're not the only one
with smooth moves, huh?

Ace bows again,
slower and more dramatic.

What?
My voice is louder than I want,
so I choke back my shriek
before I squeak out,
You think those
were smooth moves
back there?
You think I wanted *you*
to do that
to say that
to help *by taking credit*
to ruin
THE ONE TIME
I had a chance
to be invisible
on my own terms,
and stick it to
all those terrible kids
and *to Mr. Mann?*

Ace looks as surprised
as I felt
two minutes ago.

Whoa.
Ben Y.
No.
I was just trying to—

The words are flat.
Dead in my mouth:

Ruin everything?

Ace is so surprised,
eyes wide.
No!
The opposite of that!

Ben B steps between us.

It looks like Ben Y
would like you to take
three steps back,
Ace.

Jordan and Javier
join Ben B
in the blockade
between me
and Ace.

This is really weird.
And confusing.
But fine.
Okay.

Ace's palms are up,
in an *I surrender* pose,
but Ace's mouth
is not ready
to give up.

I was trying to take one for the team!
I thought you y'alls would appreciate that!
Especially you, Ben Y.
After you saved me from the Poncho of Doom . . .
I thought—

Jordan, Ben B, Javier
have been moving forward,
slowly making sure Ace
moves closer
and closer
to the door.

Jordan's voice is very low,
but I still hear him say:

You can't take one for the team if you aren't part of the team.

Ace's mouth opens,
but Jordan's words
have chased away
any words
Ace might have left
to say.

Jordan's words
chase Ace away, too,
banging out the library door
with a smash
and a crash.

□ □ □ □

So you DID do it? I knew it!
It was so good and funny! Why didn't you tell us about it?
See? T-told y you. N not my dr-drawings.

They all talk at once,
their questions
bombarding,
overlapping,
yapping,
and I can't . . .
I can't with any of it. . . .
Not right now.

I *guess* I can see
how Ace was trying to help,
but even so,
the bigger thing I see,
the blinking sign
in front of me,
is that Ace *assumed*
I needed help.
And I didn't.

I wasn't finished
soaking up the energy
and the power
and the . . .
satisfaction
of turning everything
and everyone
upside down.

I *liked* teetering on the edge
of mystery
and discovery.

I *liked* feeling the danger
of not knowing
what *I* might do next.

Ace took away
the one thing
that's made me
really happy
in a long time,
and for what?

To save me from getting suspended?
Who cares about that?

For one bright flash of a moment,
I was in control—
I held the answers—
I was saving *myself*.

I was actually saving myself.

⸱ ⸱ ⸱ ⸱

I just want to get out of here now,
away from the questions
and away from whatever it is
that Ms. J
is digesting. . . .

But where can I even go?
The library was the last safe space
I had left.

BUS STOP

Hey, Ben Y! Wait up! You seem definitely sad and mad and you're walking REALLY fast and it's okay if you don't want to talk about it because maybe you're riding a big wave of feelings and Mo says you don't always have to invite other people to ride your waves with you, I just wanted to let you know—

I'M FINE!
JUST LEAVE ME ALONE.
I DON'T WANT TO TALK ABOUT IT.
I DON'T WANT TO HEAR YOU TALK ABOUT IT.
I JUST NEED FIVE SECONDS OF QUIET, OKAY?
DO YOU EVEN KNOW WHAT QUIET MEANS?

The words dive-bomb Jordan,
stopping him in his tracks,
and I really really really
didn't mean to sound so loud
or so mad
because I'm not mad at *Jordan*,
I'm just thinking about
so many things,
and sometimes
Jordan is like
a jumping puppy

who barks
and barks
until you just
want to—

Ugh.
Jordan's eyes say everything
when they dip down,
away from me,
pointed at his feet
as he speedwalks
past me
and up the bus stairs
and charges all the way
to the back
and flings himself
into the very last seat.

□ □ □ □

For the first time ever,
I sit in the front seat.
All by myself.

OBenwhY: I don't know why I keep coming here

OBenwhY: but maybe I like to pretend

OBenwhY: or maybe I like to ask What If

OBenwhY: What if ghosts learn how to play Sandbox?

OBenwhY: I mean, we taught Ms. J how to play Sandbox, so nothing's impossible.

OBenwhY: . . .

OBenwhY: this is when you'd say, What's on your mind, grasshopper?

OBenwhY: and I'd say nothing

OBenwhY: and you'd say, You must keep coming here for something

OBenwhY: and I'd say fine, fine, you're right

OBenwhY: a little while ago on the bus, I heard a woman say to another woman:

OBenwhY: *You ever think about how you're only alive as long as someone remembers you?*

OBenwhY: Whoa, right?

OBenwhY: I miss you.

OBenwhY: But, no offense? It's starting to get hard for me to perfectly remember your face.

OBenwhY: It's getting all soft around the edges now

OBenwhY: blurring and blending into my brainclouds

OBenwhY: Brainclouds is a Jordan word for when all your thoughts get jumbled together

OBenwhY: Your head gets filled with growing brainclouds of jumbled words

OBenwhY: then some of the words have to rain out of your mouth one by one

OBenwhY: or even in storms of lots of words

OBenwhY: That's the only way to make room for more thoughts.

OBenwhY: I wish you could've met Jordan.

OBenwhY: He's about as different from me as ice cream is from

OBenwhY: a jet ski.

OBenwhY: he was nice to me today

OBenwhY: and I was kind of mean to him

OBenwhY: and I feel terrible

OBenwhY: and also I got busted doing my ananymous anonomos thing

OBenwhY: so you were right, about nothing being secret anywhere ever

OBenwhY: . . .

OBenwhY: i have so much to talk to you about,

OBenwhY: i need so much advice

OBenwhY: but i don't know where to start

OBenwhY: it's all . . . a lot. and then, on top of all that, the lady on the bus scared me.

OBenwhY: if she's right, and you're still alive until you're forgotten . . .

0BenwhY: What if I stop being able to remember the angles of your face?

0BenwhY: What if I start to forget your mahogany voice?

0BenwhY: What if that means one day *I'm* the one who accidentally kills you forever?

0BenwhY: What if I become YOUR ghostkiller?

0BenwhY: . . .

0BenwhY: . . .

0BenwhY: I *really* like the idea that you're still alive, though, somehow, in some way.

0BenwhY: My brainclouds are your oxygen.

0BenwhY: My thoughts about you are like CPR.

0BenwhY: . . .

0BenwhY: it's late and it's been a wild day and I'm not making any sense

0BenwhY: . . .

0BenwhY: . . .

SBIOBEN: makes perfect sense to me

I jump up so fast,
the chair spins across the floor,
crashing into the wall behind me.

I slam the computer off so fast,
I'm sure *it* crashes, too:
this system was improperly shut down
files may have been lost

Minds may have been lost, too.

I know it wasn't him.
It couldn't be.

It couldn't be.

I whisper it
so I can hear the words out loud,
so I can really, really believe them.

It couldn't be.

It couldn't be.

▫ ▫ ▫ ▫

But . . .

The tiny voice
from the dark shadows
in the back of my mind
slithers awake—

But . . .
But . . .
But . . .

The tiny voice gets louder,
no matter how hard I try
to fight it back,
it starts to even sing
just a little bit,
so that I can hear it louder,
and clearer
and brighter
and bigger. . . .

But . . .
But . . .
But . . .
What if . . .
What if the impossible . . .

What if the impossible just became the possible. . . .
What if the impossible just became the possible, just like
Benicio said it could?

□ □ □ □

No way.
No how.

It wasn't Benicio.
I mean, duh.
It couldn't be.
It *can't* be.
His ashes are in that box,
the one right down the hall,
on the shelf,
the center of Mom's shrine.

My stomach flips
and spins
and crashes in
on itself.

But then . . . who?
How?

Why now?

WHAT

SCHOOL

I do not love
riding bus 315
all alone.

I do not love
not talking to Jordan,
not hearing
every
single
tiny
detail
about last night's
Fierce Across America episode.

I do not love
making the long walk to school
all by myself,
not laughing
at his stories and jokes.

I do not love
not being able to find Jordan
in the halls before class.
It makes me feel wobbly,
like I've lost myself, too,
like I'm only half of me,

wandering aimlessly,
thinking half thoughts,
farting half farts.

Should I keep looking for him?
Should I leave him alone?
How can I say I'm sorry
if he's nowhere to be found?

The last time we were apart this long
was when we'd never met.

▫ ▫ ▫ ▫

Walking so slow,
not wanting to go to class,
but not wanting to go
anywhere else,
I drag by the beige globs,
I drag through the halls,
I ignore the *Ben Who What Why*s,
I listen for
DRESS CODEs.

When I pass by
the library window,
I stop for a look.
The Planet Safe Space poster

looms at me.
Still giant,
but different now.

Some of the rockets
have names on them,
and some are almost ready
to plant their one-person colonies
on the face
of Planet Safe Space.

Some of the names
are names of people
who call me *Ben Who What Why*,
who call Ace *Dress Code*,
Who like to emphasize
certain words
like *IT*
when they talk to me
like I'm not
an actual human person
with actual human person feelings.

I go into the library,
and with a quick rip,
I pull off a rocket,
accidentally tearing

the construction paper
just a bit
at the nose.

I take out my gum,
stick it on the rocket
so it fixes the tear,
and so I can stick it back
on the poster
in a much better
position.

I write my name
on the rocket
I just pointed
in the opposite direction
of all the other rockets.

Now *my* rocket is closest
to whatever adventure awaits
in *actual* safe space
far away from here.

▫ ▫ ▫ ▫

Ace catches me
on my way to class.

Brought your belt back.
From the other day.
Thanks.
It really helped . . .
bring the whole look together.

I take it without slowing down.
I'm mad at Ace in a way
I've never been mad before.

I want to scream so loud
and so long
that my head explodes.

I'll probably never
ever
have another day
where no one calls me
Ben Who What Why.
And I'll probably *keep*
having days
where all I want to do
is cry.
So, yeah.
That's probably why I'm so mad.

Whether it's fair or not,
I blame Ace
for all of the
above.

▫ ▫ ▫ ▫

And ALSO
Jordan is mad at me,
which is the worst
(and which is
technically
my own fault,
but I'm blaming Ace
for THAT, too).

▫ ▫ ▫ ▫

Ben Y?

Ace calls after me,
but I'm already around the corner,
heading to lunch.

▫ ▫ ▫ ▫

As soon as I think
enough time has passed
for Ace to
poof,
go away,
disappear,
I grab a snack
and duck out
of the loud
and smelly
lunchroom,
where I didn't see Jordan
or Ben B
or anyone
I could trust
to be nice
to me.

I jog to the library,
head to the back,
find a computer,
and . . .
my heart speeds up.

I don't like to visit the cabin
when I'm at school,
and I know it's impossible
to talk to actual Benicio,
but I want to
so badly
it almost
physically
hurts.

Maybe reading the archives will help,
for a minute anyway,
and distract me
from the Not-Benicio
in the cabin chat last night,
and whatever that's about.

BEFORE

SB1OBEN: i talked to mom today

SB1OBEN: she wasn't calling from the moon, so i guess you've forgiven her?

OBenwhY: never! i'm going to get your room one day, trust me

SB1OBEN: over my dead body, grasshopper

OBenwhY: whatever, drama 👑. you lost your room when you got 👓

SB1OBEN: ANYWAY, Mom said you got in a fight at school? What's THAT about?

OBenwhY: nothing

SB1OBEN: doesn't sound like nothing

OBenwhY: i don't really want to talk about it

SB1OBEN: 🥺

OBenwhY: uuuugggghhhhhhhhhhh fine.

OBenwhY: But you stay there.

OBenwhY: I'm going to build a teeny tiny mini planet with starstone and go up there

OBenwhY: I need to feel the world at my feet for a minute

OBenwhY: if I'm going to talk about this AGAIN

OBenwhY: cause I've been talking about it with mom for houuurrrrsssss.

SB10BEN: 😊

SB10BEN: how does it feel to know you can build your very own place in space AND have the world at your feet any time you want?

OBenwhY: it feels like i want to feel that way IRL, not just in Sandbox

OBenwhY: Boom! Look how fast I built my tiny planet! How does it feel to look up to ME for once. 😉

SB10BEN: I like your avatar's shoes, btw. Nice red.

OBenwhY: Thanks.

SB10BEN: So. Now that you're officially over everything (har har), you want to talk about what happened at school?

OBenwhY: Here's the thing . . . if I wear red shoes, that doesn't mean I hate blue shoes

SB1OBEN: uh, yes? correct?

OBenwhY: I don't even hate OTHER people who wear blue shoes

OBenwhY: I'm just a person who likes red shoes.

OBenwhY: I mean, it's not like anyone has to wear ONLY blue shoes or ONLY red shoes.

OBenwhY: Isn't there room in the world for all colors of shoes? No color is better than another.

OBenwhY: And no one should tell me what color to wear.

OBenwhY: you don't get to make fun of me for wearing shoes when you ALSO WEAR SHOES

OBenwhY: They're just shoes!

SB1OBEN: Hey, grasshopper . . . are we still talking about shoes, or—

OBenwhY: We're all just shoes!

OBenwhY: Or wait . . . maybe we're all feet?

SB1OBEN: And all feet are equal no matter what shoes they wear?

OBenwhY: YES! Except . . . my feet aren't equal.

SB1OBEN: Huh?

OBenwhY: I have eleven toes, remember?

OBenwhY: My feet are literally not equal. 😄

SB10BEN: Well, no wonder you stand apart. 😄

OBenwhY: grooooaaaaannnn 😄

SB10BEN: So that's what the fight was about? Your shoes?

OBenwhY: well it was about why do people think they're better than me, when really we're all—

CHAT INFRACTION

OBenwhY: what was THAT?

OBenwhY: What does chat infraction even mean? it kind of sounds like something a teacher would yell in a libr—

CHAT INFRACTION

OBenwhY: HEY! Make it stop. That's super annoying.

SB10BEN: oh, whoops. I forgot I added in the new code.

SB10BEN: Something new I've been working on. No more than 100 characters per line in chat.

SB10BEN: You should know, on your third infraction you get ejected from chat and you have a 30 min respawn perio—

CHAT INFRACTION

OBenwhY: omg

OBenwhY: this is the dumbest thing I've ever seen

OBenwhY: why are you working on this?

SB10BEN: the money guys want to increase game play and decrease chat. they say you can chat anywhere, but yo

CHAT INFRACTION

OBenwhY: blah blah blerg blerg grown-up talk 😴

SB10BEN: WOW that is annoying.

OBenwhY: grown-up talk or chat infractions? Answer: BOTH

OBenwhY: can't you just tell them this is a dumb idea?

OBenwhY: 100% of players who've tested it hate it. 👎

SB10BEN: I wish I could, but I but I sold my soul to the 😈 and now I do what the 😈 says in exchange for the 😈's money.

SB10BEN: that's why i built this cabin, so at least I have SOME way to keep creating cool things. I hate that wo—

CHAT INFRACTION

SB1OBEN HAS BEEN EJECTED FROM GAME

THIRTY MINUTE RESPAWN COUNTDOWN BEGINS NOW

OBenwhY: omg HARSH

OBenwhY: but not as harsh as when I use my red shoes to kick your butt and steal your bedroom over your dead—

CHAT INFRACTION

OBENWHY HAS BEEN EJECTED FROM GAME

THIRTY MINUTE RESPAWN COUNTDOWN BEGINS NOW

THE LIBRARY

That helped a little,
but it didn't quiet
the whispering,
taunting
What if . . .
What if . . .
What if . . .
that's still
echoing
in the back
of my mind.

I click away from the archive
and into live chat.

Not-Benicio
probably won't be here
at the exact time
I have lunch,
but what if . . .
what if . . .
what if . . .
what if I get some

actual
Benicio
advice
right now
when I need it
the most?

□ □ □ □

Besides, it wouldn't be the first time
I stared at a blinking cursor
while I ate some chips
and wished
for the impossible
to be possible.

NOW

0BenwhY: Hello?

0BenwhY: Not-Benicio?

0BenwhY: Any chance you're around?

0BenwhY: Any chance you're actually Benicio?

0BenwhY: Or his ghost?

0BenwhY: jk, i know you're not

0BenwhY: i know that's impossible

0BenwhY: anyway

0BenwhY: If you *are* around, I have twenty minutes, a bag of chips, and a LOT of questions.

SBiOBEN: What kind of chips?

0BenwhY: 😑

SBiOBEN: I'm not a ghost.

SBiOBEN: I read the chat log from last time

SBiOBEN: you were saying something about a ghost

SBiOBEN: i'm not Benicio, either

SBiOBEN: i don't even know who that is

0BenwhY: Thank you for confirming that, Not-Benicio, Not-Ghost.

OBenwhY: though any person with a brain knows ghosts aren't real

OBenwhY: and what do you mean you read the chat log?

SBIOBEN: just from when you were in the cabin last night. not the whole archive.

SBIOBEN: that would be super rude and none of my business.

OBenwhY: WHO ARE YOU AND HOW DO YOU KEEP GETTING IN THIS CABIN????

OBenwhY: I AM VERY CRANKY AND I WANT ANSWERS.

OBenwhY: . . .

OBenwhY: ?????????????????????

SBIOBEN: I just wanted to talk to you. I want to talk to you right now. That's why I came back.

OBenwhY: that does not answer my question

SBIOBEN: trust me. i'm a good person. who is not a ghost. who wants to chat.

SBIOBEN: what is this? squishy iron? what can you build with squishy iron?

OBenwhY: I KNOW YOU'RE NOT A GHOST.

OBenwhY: you don't have to keep saying it and saying it.

OBenwhY: the more you say it, the more i think maybe you're NOT a good person

OBenwhY: maybe you're a creeper

OBenwhY: and that isn't squishy iron, it's an Indestructible Cloud Block

SBIOBEN: what do you build with an Indestructible Cloud Block?

OBenwhY: obviously, if you were Benicio's ghost, you would know.

SBIOBEN: as I said

SBIOBEN: I am not a ghost.

OBenwhY: so that only leaves one other option.

OBenwhY: you're a creeper

SBIOBEN: i'm not a creeper

OBenwhY: that's exactly what a creeper would say

SBIOBEN: Good point.

SBIOBEN: I'm not a gross internet person, I promise. I'm not a gross real-life person, either.

SBIOBEN: And I'm sorry your brother died.

SBIOBEN: That is a really 💩 thing to happen.

OBenwhY: Yeah.

OBenwhY: . . .

SBIOBEN: I would be a horrible person if I actually pretended to be his ghost.

OBenwhY: Agreed.

SBIOBEN: I would never do anything like that.

OBenwhY: except you ARE somehow using his avatar
OBenwhY: So you can see how this definitely isn't traumatic at all.
OBenwhY: To be chatting with him, even though it isn't him.
OBenwhY: Not confusing or weird or anything.
OBenwhY: not like we're in some movie and it turns out he didn't die at all,
OBenwhY: he was actually kidnapped by bad guys who thought he was someone else
OBenwhY: and he's spent all these months earning his kidnappers' trust
OBenwhY: so they've finally given him a crappy old computer
OBenwhY: to play games on
OBenwhY: and he's hacked into their internet
OBenwhY: so he can come here to our private server
OBenwhY: to tell me he's alive.

SBIOBEN: Well NOW I feel like a jerk

OBenwhY: and yet you claim to be a good person

OBenwhY: a good nice person would tell me how they got in here

SBЮBEN: I . . .

SBЮBEN: Sorry. I have to go.

OBenwhY: right. of course you do.

STILL IN THE LIBRARY

The bell beeps its ring,
so I grab my backpack,
and breathe deep,
looking for Jordan,
Javier, and Ben B
in the streaming
hallway.

Ben Y?
Can you hang back for a second?
I'll give you a pass to class.

Ms. J
floats and billows over,
gesturing to her office.

Do I even have a choice?

I just nod.
Okay.

▫ ▫ ▫ ▫

When the door shuts,
Ms. J exhales slowly,
like she's been holding her breath
for a very, very long time.

She opens a desk drawer
and pulls out
a jar of gummy bears.
She offers it to me.
I take a couple
(red and orange)
but my mouth is too dry
to eat them.

Ms. J takes a handful herself,
munching while she talks.

Here's the deal, Ben Y.
I know it wasn't Ace.
I know it was you.
The Unauthorized Hart Times?
You flew by the library
early that morning
flinging papers in your wake
like a . . .
like a . . .
like I don't even know what!

I burst out with:
There's no way you saw me!
All the teachers were in a meeting!
The coast was clear!

My words trail off
as I realize
I just fell in
the most obvious trap
ever.

Ms. J shrugs,
smiles kindly.

Sorry, my friend.
Totally outmaneuvered you there.

She eats a red gummy bear.
Thinks for a minute.
Shakes her head.

Now that THAT is out of way,
and I really do know it was you,
I need you to listen to me.
This could mean big-time trouble, kiddo.

And we're going to need
to work together
to try to prevent that.
Okay?

I nod,
my mouth too dry
for gummy bears
OR words.

You know
and I know
getting suspended?
That's not going to teach you anything.

I open my mouth,
prepped and ready to say:
I don't really care about
getting suspended.

But she holds up her Stop hand
before I can say anything.

You might think you don't care.
But I care.
In fact, I care enough to try my best to teach you to care.
Getting punished for years to come
because of a flag on your record?

No way I'm letting that happen.
But we need to figure out a way
to make certain . . .
other adults
in this school
understand that, too.

I make a note
to remember how
she said *we.*
Not *you.*
More than one time.

While I don't approve of your tactics,
and I need you to understand
what you did was quite wrong. . . .

She chews more gummy bears,
rocks in her chair
just a little bit
and smiles at me.

You really did the whole thing
all by yourself?

I nod.
She nods.
Her smile gets a little bit bigger.

On a certain level,
I'm quite impressed.
The effort you invested,
the skills you used,
the drive it took
to draft and print and distribute,
and, wow, Ben Y . . .
your spelling has REALLY improved.

A smile creeps across my face
even though my eyes
stay glued
to Ms. J's desk.

I'm so sorry you felt like
you needed to do this.
I'm so sorry it came to that.

Her laser eyes
drag my unsure eyes
up from her desk
so she can show me
she means what she says.

So . . . I'm not in trouble, then?
My voice is almost a whisper.

Ms. J sucks her bottom lip
for just a second
before she says,
You're not NOT in trouble.
But we'll take care of this in-house,
as they say.

I . . .
I don't know what that means.

Ms. J stands,
opens the door,
motions me out.

That's okay,
she says,
as I shakily stand up.
You'll understand soon enough.

I grab my backpack,
unsure of what exactly to think
about today,
about this moment,
about anything.

And hey, Ben Y?
Ms. J catches me
just before

I get to the door.
Her voice is soft.
So are her eyes.

Please understand,
while I'm not proud of your choices,
I am proud of you.
You got the whole school talking
about what YOU felt was important.
You pointed out glaring hypocrisies
that everyone should notice.

I don't know what to say.
I don't know where to look.
The tops of my ears burn.
In a good way.
The bottom of my stomach melts.
In a good way.

I promise to help you use your powers for good, not evil.
But more than that, I promise to just . . . help.
The points you made,
while crude,
were valid.
And we'll work together
to follow the proper channels
to get your voice heard.
Okay?

I nod,
not sure what to say.

She hands me a folded piece of paper.

Here's something to help you . . .
research . . .
your authorized admin profile article.
Take a look at it tonight.
We can talk more tomorrow.

I walk out the door
as I choke out,
Okay,
and I feel something
expanding in my chest,
filling up the hollow parts.

Ms. J saw what I did, sure,
but also?
She saw what I *meant* to do.
She saw my words,
but she saw *me*, too.

THE BUS

Jordan is still gone
like *he's* a ghost,
so I walk to the bus stop
all alone.

The humid evening heat
soaks into me
and the hot wind
presses into me,
an unrelenting weight,
wearing me down

There's someone ahead,
standing at the corner,
waiting for the bus.

And as I get closer
and the person gets taller
and I realize it isn't Jordan,
the pressing wind
goes from heavy
to suffocating,
stealing my breath
with every hot gust.

▫ ▫ ▫ ▫

Hey.

Ace's wave arcs though the air,
like a rainbow
and it feels like
a hundred
a thousand
a million
years ago
when all I wanted
was for Ace
to notice me.

Now I just need
a few
Ace-free
seconds
or minutes
or days
or weeks
to sort out
what I think.

□ □ □ □

I'm afraid my face
might have done a thing
when I realized Ace
was not Jordan,
and I'm also afraid
Ace saw the thing
my face did,
and I don't want to
explain my face
or anything else
to Ace
right now.

I drop my backpack
and toss myself onto the bench,
pulling my knees up to my chest
so my legs don't fry
on the burning seat.

Ace flops down next to me,
legs protected by
very light pink camo tights
underneath
black basketball shorts.

Neither of us says anything.

▫ ▫ ▫ ▫

You know,
I say,
finally,
feeling the words
slide out
on their own.

If you want to be
a good friend,
or even just
a friend at all,
and if you want to
find a way
to be part of the team . . .
maybe you could . . .
stop trying so hard?

Maybe I should hope that didn't sound mean.
A small part of me wants it to, though.
And based on the way
Ace's face
lost about fifty percent
of its usual shining gleam
I'm pretty sure
that small part of myself
just got what it wants.

Was that rude?
Just . . .
maybe . . .
help us,
help me,
get to know you?
A little?

You're always hanging out,
and making jokes,
and being cool,
but who ARE you, Ace?

What's left of the gleam
dims in Ace's eyes.

But
don't you remember
what YOU said
when you saved me
on the poncho day?
Ace whispers.
I'm a You.
You're a Me.

The bus is pulling up.
I stand first,
and look down
at Ace
looking up
at me,
eyes big
and confused.

Yes, you're a Me
and I'm a You,
but that's like,
a deep-down thing
to know,
you know?

You can be a Me
and I can be a You
but that still doesn't mean
I know all your thoughts and feelings,
or you know all of mine,
you know what I mean?

You can say you y'alls
and newspapering
and borrow
all the Jordan words

you want,
but that doesn't make you
a friend, *Ace.*

It just makes you a chameleon.

□ □ □ □

We stay quiet
all the way to my stop
until I stand up,
make my way to the door,
and Ace whispers,

Valid point, grasshopper.
You're really good at those.

□ □ □ □

And all of the one million
billion
trillion
things
that happened today
or this week
or this year
or ever
melt into one

burning lava blob
of a thought
that sizzles and sparks
behind my eyes
and threatens to
burn away
any other thought
I've ever had
or ever will have:

Ace just called me
grasshopper.

□ □ □ □

Only one person *ever* called me that.
Only one.

When Benicio first left home,
after he got his GED,
and he and Paul and Juanita
drove all the way
across the country
in his busted-up Bronco
and they somehow got money
to start this new company
that made a game
called Sandbox . . .

and after the money guys
set them up
in a fancy office
in a tall building
with as many snacks
as you could imagine,

and after Benicio
missed coming home for Christmas
twice
and practically lived at work,
making Sandbox bigger and better,

and after Paul quit to marry Juanita,
and after Juanita quit to marry Paul,
Benicio kept working
and stayed so far away
and wouldn't let me take his bedroom
even though that was stupid,
because we both knew
he was big and old
and never coming back . . .

and after he let me test out Sandbox
before anyone else,
after he taught me how to create an avatar,
after he taught me how to mix potions,
after he taught me how to build things

without worrying
about being wrong,
because—

Wait for it, Benita!
There is no wrong in Sandbox!
How about THAT!—

After alllllllll of that,
I finally got up the guts
to trust him with something
I never trusted anyone with
ever before,
because if he could trust me,
I could trust him, right?
And I asked him if he could make a potion,
just for my avatar,
a transformation potion
that would let me be a girl one day
and a boy another day
and both some other day
and neither whenever I wanted,
and he said,
Sure, okay.
And I made him say again
the thing about how
nothing can be wrong in Sandbox

because there are no mistakes,
and he asked if I ever felt like a mistake,
like, in real life,
and I said not really
and he said not *really*
and I said only on bad days
and he said you're not a mistake, kiddo.
People aren't mistakes *ever*, okay?
Not in Sandbox and *definitely* not in real life.
And I said okay
and he said okay,
and a couple of days later,
he created the cabin just for us,
so we could talk and create
all on our own,
and he showed me the transformation potion
and said he was still working on it
but I could test it anyway, try *this*,
so I tried *that*,
and *that* made me jump
as high as the sun
and then past the sun
and all the way to the Sandbox moon
and back again,
and Benicio typed,
Look at you.

To the moon and back again.
How did it feel to have the whole world at your feet?
And I said it felt like being a grasshopper.
And he typed, *HAHAHAHA.*
Then he typed, *Did it feel like anything else, grasshopper?*
And I typed, *It made me feel free.*
And he typed, *Perfect.*
I love you to the moon and back, grasshopper.
I want YOU to love you to the moon and back, too.
I want you to always feel free to be the You you are.

▫ ▫ ▫ ▫

And then he called me on the actual phone
and I cried a little bit,
which sounds weird,
but wasn't.

▫ ▫ ▫ ▫

And the friends I have now
never knew Benicio
called me grasshopper
because they never knew Benicio.

That is another thought
I tuck away
in my brainclouds . . .
something to think
a *lot* more about
some other time,
if I'm ever able to
think about anything
other than this thing,
which is that

Ace
called me grasshopper.

Ace did.

Ace.

#

0BenwhY: hi, creeper

SBЮBEN: creeper? come on! I thought we sorted that out.

0BenwhY: we have sorted nothing out.

SBЮBEN: Is this about me having to disappear before?
SBЮBEN: i lost track of time and was about to be in big trouble
SBЮBEN: anyway. that's a boring story.
SBЮBEN: how are you? Long time no talk.

0BenwhY: *has* it been a long time?

SBЮBEN: what do you mean?

0BenwhY: I mean, it feels like we JUST had a chat

SBЮBEN: can't stop thinking about me, huh? ☺

OBenwhY: well you ARE still impersonating my dead brother

OBenwhY: it's hard not to think about that

OBenwhY: also, I think you're reading the chat archives

OBenwhY: none of those things are great ways to get me to like you here OR irl

SBIOBEN: very fair point, and also that makes me sound like a huge turd

OBenwhY: because you are acting like a huge turd

OBenwhY: tell me who you are.

SBIOBEN: Not until you've had some time to get to know me. And like me.

SBIOBEN: Plus, I think you already know.

OBenwhY: tell me who you are.

SBIOBEN: I think you already know.

OBenwhY: TELL ME WHO YOU ARE

SBIOBEN: I THINK YOU ALREADY KNOW. I'VE BEEN LEAVING CLUES.

OBenwhY: anything can be a clue if you want it to be

OBenwhY: Everything can be a clue if you want it to be

SBIOBEN: More fair points. You're good at those.

OBenwhY: stop trying to change the subject every time I ask who you are

OBenwhY: 😫 I have to go before I get mad

SBIOBEN: noooo! you're getting mad?? Why??

SBIOBEN: i thought we were bantering . . . joking around

OBenwhY: that's what you want me to like about you?

OBenwhY: how funny you think you are in chat????? While you're, like, Sandbox-cosplaying my dead brother????????

OBenwhY: if you can't figure out why that makes me mad . . . argh!

OBenwhY: make sure to go back and read THIS chat archive while you're reading all the rest

OBenwhY: bet you'll figure it out

OBenwhY: also, DON'T actually read the chat archives. Those are private.

OBenwhY HAS EXITED GAME

HOME

You're in here again?
Is this your room now, or something?

Esme stands in the doorway,
watching me wipe my eyes
as I turn off Benicio's computer.

Do you still have my markers?
Her chirps are unsure
as she looks me over,
trying to figure out
what's going on.

I shake my head.
No markers.

I give her my best smile,
which is only a sideways half smile
because my face can't catch up
to all my different feelings
right now.

You should come in.

I stand up
then flop myself
fast and bouncy
onto Benicio's bed.
His pillow is still missing.

It's okay.
He wouldn't mind.

Esme squints,
shakes her head.
We both know
if he were alive
he would probably
still be dumb
about letting anyone go into
his room.

Well, hey.
I give her a jokey half smile
and a giant shrug.
At least he can't get mad anymore.

Esme thinks about this
like it's *not* a really bad attempt
at a really bad non-joke,
and she nods,
very seriously,

before she bolts
into the room,
crashing into me,
linking her arms
around my neck
and whispering into my ear,
He can't be mad,
but he still loves us, right?

I don't have a lot of answers,
but this is one answer
I do know.

My squeeze tells her
just how right
I know she is.

□ □ □ □

This day
has been a thousand days,
a million years,
a forever plus infinity
and I'm so so so tired.

But when I *want* to sleep,
it stays just out of my reach,
like in those movies

with hallways
that stretch and stretch,
fooling you into thinking
the exit door is right there,
even though it's always
not quite ever there.

I can't stop thinking about Ace
and the bus
and the grasshopper
and the chat I had with Not-Benicio tonight
and the last chat I ever had with Real Benicio
and the thing is,
I know I ask a lot of questions
and I know I complain
when I don't have answers,
but right now,
even though
I'm pretty sure
I have the answer
to a really big question,
I kind of wish
I didn't.

□ □ □ □

There's no use trying to sleep,
so I climb off my bunk,
sneak past Esme,
who chirps
even in her sleep,
and into Benicio's room
where I left my backpack
when I got home from school.

I pull out the folded sheet
Ms. J gave me,
to help me research
my authorized admin profile,
and I sit at Benicio's desk,
turning on the lamp
that looks like
a Sandbox torch.

It's a page
from an old *Hart Times*
with a few things circled . . .
and . . .
ooooh.
Whoa.
Is this what she meant?
About paying attention?

We were all so busy laughing
at *Jordan's Hot Takes*
and Ms. J's giant glasses
that we missed this,
completely.

Malcolm Mann.
Deputy Editor.
Not bald yet.
No mustache yet.
But those eyes don't lie.
It's him.
For sure.

And the title of his column?

"Fight the Mann:
Students' Rights are Human Rights."

▫ ▫ ▫ ▫

WHAT.

< NEWSPAPER TYPING CLUB CHAT >

JJ11347: Whoa whoa wow! What happened in here? I hardly recognize this place!

BenBee: shiitake mushrooms! WHO did all of this?

jajajavier:): Look at this over here!
jajajavier:): hahaha, check it out!
jajajavier:): the sign says LOUD ROOM instead of STUDY ROOM.
jajajavier:): You can blow stuff up in here! Cool!

BenBee: And look at this! It's like that accidental chickenfall I made once, but with books.

jajajavier:): A bookfall! 😄 Don't stand at the bottom of it. 💀

JORDANJMAGEDDON!!!!!: A library really CAN be magical. Just like you said, Ms. J.

JJ11347: Oh, you y'alls.

BenBee: seriously, though. Who built all of this?
BenBee: OBenwhY, *you're* super quiet.

Who's ready for some Newspapering?
Ace's voice echoes toward us
as an Ace-shaped blur runs top speed
through the library,
interrupting our chat,
making us look up,
eyeballs peering over monitors
like we're all . . .
what are those animals
that peek their eyes
out of the holes in the ground
where they live?
Prairie dogs?
Like that.

PlanetSafeAce ENTERS GAME

JJ11347: Hello, Ace. Nice of you to join us . . . THIRTY minutes late.

PlanetSafeAce: Sorry about that, Ms. J.
PlanetSafeAce: dress coded AGAIN. I told Mr. Mann to talk to you
PlanetSafeAce: like you said to do
PlanetSafeAce: I hope that's ok

JJ11347: Absolutely ok, Ace. Thank you for listening to me.

PlanetSafeAce: Hi, everybody.

OBenwhY: someone better take credit for all this cool stuff, before Ace does

JJ11347: Ben Y!

jajajavier:): Hi, Ace.

JORDANJMAGEDDON!!!!: 🙄

JJ11347: Jordan!

JORDANJMAGEDDON!!!!: sorry. my hand slipped on the keyboard.

JJ11347: Time for some newspapering, everyone.

JJ11347: Those authorized articles aren't going to write themselves.

JJ11347: Let's save and exit and get to work.

jajajavier:): Aw, really?? But there's still a bunch of new stuff we haven't even checked out yet.

JORDANJMAGEDDON!!!!: hahaha, get it?? Checked out?? And we're in a library?? 🖐🖐

PlanetSafeAce: 🖐🖐

JORDANJMAGEDDON!!!!: that high five was for Javi

PlanetSafeAce: oh. sorry.

Ms. J stands,
smoothing her caftan.

Ben Y.
Can I see you for a second?

□ □ □ □

Ms. J tilts her head,
resting her giant hoop earring
on her turquoise shoulder
as she sneaks her way
into looking at my face.

Did you look at the . . .
research . . .
I provided?
For your authorized article?

I . . .
Uh . . .

A smile sneaks
to the corners
of my mouth.

I did.

Her eyes catch mine,
holding them
for just a second
so I can see
the sparks.

And?
she asks.
Did you prepare some questions?
We're staring down a deadline, so . . .
how about we go
conduct
that
interview?!

She looks excited
and maybe angry?
But not angry with me.

I think.

□ □ □ □

Shouldn't we, like—
call first or something?

My heartbeat doubles
at the thought of
walking right into
Mr. Mann's office.
That's like
walking right into
the belly of a beast.

Are we even allowed to . . .
just . . .
show up . . .
in Mr. Mann's office?
He's always in the halls.
How are we supposed to find him?
Unless . . .
we could use Ace as bait.
Haha.
Sorry.
Not funny.

I keep talking
because there's no way,
no way,
I can tell her
I don't have any questions.

Ms. J's face looks pointy,
flashing,
almost like Benicio's
when he knew
he was starting an argument
just for the fun of it.

We will NOT be using anyone
as bait.
We WILL be using
your smart questions
and journalistic intuition.
Ready?
Let's go!

I nod.
I hold my breath,
feeling my heart pound.

I'm sure I can think of some questions, right?
I mean, that IS my specialty.

◦ ◦ ◦ ◦

We walk down the hall,
and it's like her swooshing caftan
carries us both
on a breathless breeze.

I can't believe you both
went to school here,
I manage to stammer
as we blow through
hallway
after hallway.

Ms. J slows her pace, nodding.

Malcolm Mann,
Hart Times
Deputy Editor,
and I . . .
we go way back.

The sparks
from Ms. J's eyes
turn to bursting fireworks.

It feels a little bit
(or maybe a lotta bit)
like Ms. J wishes she
was the one
about to conduct
the Malcolm Mann Admin Profile.

▫ ▫ ▫ ▫

As we wait
to get called back
to Mr. Mann's office,
a thought pierces my brain.
Maybe it's weird
this never occurred to me
before I saw all those old
Hart Times circa 1988,
but:

Ms. J was *my age* once.

She lived in this town
as a *kid*
like *me*.

Maybe she rode the 315.
Maybe she hated gym.
Maybe she waded through beige
every day
and dreamed
of swimming through
sparkles and rainbows
instead.

How could she *not* dream of that?
How could she *not* plan her escape?
How could she *still* be here?
Still working on the *Hart Times*?
Now??
A hundred thousand years AFTER
1988???
Still spending nearly every day
looking into the weasel face
of Malcolm Mann,
former Deputy Editor,
current
[fart noise]????

□ □ □ □

A shiver
spills down
my spine
as I wonder,

Will *I* still live here,
in this
same small town
when *I* am
as old
as Ms. J?

Will *I* still be
a Hart Rocket,
never blasting off
to a new world
or a new life
or a new anything?

Will I still have to face
[insert name of anyone
from the beige blob
here]
nearly
every
day?

I shudder
like I just drank
orange juice
after brushing my teeth.

⌐ ⌐ ⌐ ⌐

Well, HELLO.
Mr. Mann stands
in the doorway
leading back
to all the admin offices.

What a . . .
lovely SURPRISE.
Ms. Jackson,
MX. Ybarra,
come on BACK.

I throw a look at Ms. J
that says,
This feels like a terrible idea.

Ms. J throws a look at me
that says,
This is about to be an ADVENTURE.

And I don't know how
she can make fun of him
with only her eyes,
but she does,
and it makes me relax,
just enough
to almost make me
smile.

◌ ◌ ◌ ◌

Thank you for seeing us,
Mal— Mr. Mann.

Mr. Mann leans back,
his chair squeaking,
his eyes narrowing.

We won't take up too much time.
Ben Y has some questions for you.
For the—
authorized—
admin profile.
Ms. J continues.
Her voice is
as easy-breezy
as her caftan.
I thought I'd tag along
to listen in.
Take it away, Ben Y.

They both stare at me.

I stare at my hands,
which miraculously hold
both a pencil
and a piece of paper.
When did *that* happen?

Uh.
I clear my throat.
The paper in front of me is blank.
I close my eyes.
I think of all the questions
crashing into each other
between the walls
of my skull
last night,
when I saw
the old article
about students' rights
being human rights,
and how Malcom Mann,
Deputy Editor
of the *Hart Times*
circa 1988,
seemed to be . . .
a nice
and thoughtful
kid.

If I reach out
and grab one,
just one

of those questions,
which one
will it

What happened *to you?*

I blurt out,
not realizing
how loud
my voice will be
as I immediately
lose control
over all the other questions
that tumble out
next.

Like, for real?

Ms. J clears her throat,
taps her shoe against mine,
but I can't stop now.
This storm has been brewing
for a really long time,
and you can't cram
booming thunder
back into the clouds
once it lets loose.

Did space aliens steal your soul?

My voice keeps getting louder,
but no one tells me to be quiet.
Mr. Mann seems stunned,
like he's trapped in MY web
of questions
for once.

I read this article.

I pull the folded *Hart Times*
circa 1988
out of my pocket
and spread it out
on his desk
in front of him.

I read a LOT of these articles.
And trust me,
I HATE to read.
But I read them all.
You know why?

I point at the blurry picture
of Malcom Mann's
thirteen-year-old
face.

Because I couldn't believe
THIS kid.
This NICE kid
could
POSSIBLY
be you.
But it is, isn't it?
And you wrote this article, didn't you?
It says right here that you—
YOU—
were worried about students feeling safe at school?
Like you say you are now?
Except . . . you aren't worried about me feeling safe, are you?
Or Ace?
You do know our clothes literally can't hurt anyone, right?

I glance at Ms. J.
She is not smiling.
She isn't even blinking.
She's staring at Mr. Mann.
Hard.

Maybe that's why her eyes
are watering
like that.

Were YOU bullied in middle school, Mr. Mann?
Is that why you became a vice principal?
So you could stop bullies?
Or so you could become one?

Ms. J's head whips around
at exactly the same time
my hand flies up,
covering my mouth
and Mr. Mann growls,
ENOUGH.

He leans forward in his seat now,
clasping his hands
on his desk,
almost like
he's about to start
praying.
Or *preying?*

I'm SORRY,
but I thought
BENITA—

excuse me—
MX. Ybarra,
was here
to APOLOGIZE
for the
INSULTING missive
she used to DISRUPT
the ENTIRE school.

There's a long pause.
No one says anything.
Mr. Mann's eyes flash,
and he smiles just a little bit.
It's the combo punch stare
grown-ups are so good at:
simmering danger,
camouflaged with a smile
that really means
Caution: danger ahead.

He points his next words
directly at me:

I SHAN'T respond
to ANY questions
until I get the APOLOGY
I DESERVE.

Ms. J blinks
about fifty-five times
like she's trying to blink back
rage lasers
from shooting out
and frying Mr. Mann
right there
in front of us.

No, I'M sorry.
she says,
through gritted teeth.

We have a deadline to meet
if we are to get this
ADMIN-APPROVED
newspaper out on time.

Ben Y is currently working on the
AUTHORIZED article
profiling YOU
that YOU
requested.

She takes a deep
deep
breath,
like she's breathing in

all the air in the room
so she can blow it out
like dragon fire.

The other matter is . . .
still under investigation.
And it will be
for quite some time,
I'm afraid,
as there are no witnesses
to the . . .
creation . . .
of the anonymous work.

Ms. J smiles politely.
There it is again.
Caution: danger ahead.

Mr. Mann opens his mouth.
He shuts it again.
He smiles at me,
like maybe
he wants to eat me.

MX. Ybarra?
Could you step into the hall for a moment?
I need to speak with Ms. Jackson.
Privately.

I leap up,
dash out,
and try not to feel guilty
for leaving
Ms. J in there
all by herself.

□ □ □ □

I mean,
have you ever *seen* a snake
unhinge its jaw
to eat an egg
or a mouse?

That's what I'm worried is happening
right now
as I hear muffled shouts
coming from
behind the closed door
of Mr. Mann's office.

□ □ □ □

Ms. J swings open the door,
motions for me to go go go,
so I go go go

and we are out of the front office,
breezing back to the library
before I can even ask:

Did he unhinge his jaw?
Or did you?

◻ ◻ ◻ ◻

As we walk past
the Planet Safe Space poster,
I manage to ask,

What happened?
Back there?
Am I still writing the profile, or . . . ?

Ms. J whips around,
says nothing.
Then . . .

That was a little . . .
MORE
than I expected, Ben Y,
in terms of . . .
an interview.

I open my mouth
to let reasons
(and excuses)
tumble out,
but she holds up
her *Stop* hand
so I shut my mouth again
and stay quiet.

Mr. Mann,
well,
he didn't enjoy your
interviewing . . .
style.

And while he admits that, yes,
he is requiring *the admin profile,*
he is now, frustratingly,
refusing to agree
to the required interview,
unless . . .
until . . .
well . . .

She sighs deeply,
gazing up at the ceiling
as if the answers

might fall from
the dusty
AC duct.

Why don't you just . . .
continue using
the old Hart Times
as research
for your Admin Spotlight.

This newspaper is coming out,
if I have to print it
my own hooverdamself.

I nod.
She nods.

For a minute,
neither of us
says anything else,
both lost
in our thoughts.

▫ ▫ ▫ ▫

You know how
a cartoon character
has a dark scribble

floating over their head
when they get mad
or frustrated?

I'm pretty sure,
if I squint right now,
I can see
an extra-scribbly scribble
vibrating
over Ms. J's
already
vibrating
pouf of a ponytail.

Get to work, Ben Y.
The time is nigh.

I don't know what that means,
but I nod anyway
and I jog away
before I get tangled up
in that expanding
angry scribble.

￼ ￼ ￼ ￼

Jordan, Javier, Ben B
huddle around a table
as Javier draws fast,
his deep chuckles
making Jordan giggle
and Ben B cackle,
and none of them look up
to see me as I walk past,
heading to the stacks
to read as many
circa 1988 *Hart Times*
as I can find.

Ace waves a book at me,
and I think
if Ace thinks
waving a book
is the way
to get me to come over,
then Ace
really doesn't know me
at all.

□ □ □ □

Ace appears in the stacks,
watching me dig through
a million *Hart Times.*

My article is almost done.
How's yours coming along?
Need any help?

I don't look up.
Nope.

◦ ◦ ◦ ◦

A wave of curls
turns toward me,
the fresh-mint smile
looks serious,
then falters
for just a second,
like a tightrope walker
who wobbles
but doesn't fall.

Question for you:
I don't, uh, guess you speak Russian, do you?

My faces scrunches up,
saying huh?
before my mouth
can catch up.

Out of all the questions
I would guess Ace might ask,
THAT was not one of them,
not even in the top
billion.

I definitely do not speak Russian.

There's a long pause
and I wonder if maybe
Ace is speaking some kind of code
I don't understand.

My mom is a professor.
Ace's fingers drum on the book.
She teaches Russian history, so
there are a lot of Russian books
all over my house.
I don't know enough Russian to read them,
but Mom taught me the Cyrillic alphabet.

What is Ace talking about?

Sorry . . . what are you talking about?
The what alphabet?

Ace blinks for a long time,
summoning something.
Patience?
Courage?
A nap?

I know you're busy writing your article, but . . .
Can you log into your cabin right now?
So I can show you how I did it?
And maybe you can forgive me?
For that, at least?
And maybe at least half
of all the uncomfortable weirdness can stop?
And maybe we can be friends?
Even if it's just half friends?
To start?

▫ ▫ ▫ ▫

It's like Ace just dumped ice water
over my head
and down my back
and into my shoes.

I try not to gasp.
But I do.

□ □ □ □

My last secret hope
flutters out
from the shadows of my guts,
exploding bright within my chest,
making me gasp shallow breaths
that darken the edges of my sight,
because of course
of course
I believed Benicio that night.
He said he would be right back.
Why wouldn't he be back?

And it's a million years later
and he never came back,
not until the other night in our chat,
and now Ace is staring at me,
not smiling anymore,
but eyes still sparkling
because I don't think Ace can ever
not sparkle.

And I close my eyes,
my turn for a long blink,
so I can really feel the feelings,
so I can ride the one last wave
of hope as it crashes
and dies
and fades away.

I've always known.
But now I *really* know.

Ace reaches over
and squeezes my hand,
quickly and just once,
and now I'm riding a new wave,
new feelings
I don't recognize
or understand.

I open my eyes.
Ace's smile wobbles again.
It's a softer, quiet smile.
No 24-carat shine,
no teeth-whitening commercial.

I want to jump up.
I want to run
and run
and run
until I get ahead
of the feelings,
the waves,
the deafening roar
of everything
crashing toward me.

I don't run, though.
I stay.

And I say,
We have to wait.

And Ace says,
Wait?

And I say,
Until Newspaper Typing Club is over.
I don't want anyone thinking we're playing Sandbox,
and I don't want to explain—

And Ace says,
Okay.

And we stay at the table,
far away
from everyone,
and we don't work on anything
and we don't say anything
and we don't look at each other,
and we wait.

< NOT FUN CHAT >

PlanetSafeAce: the Cyrillic alphabet has a lot of cool letters our alphabet doesn't have

OBenwhY: . . .

PlanetSafeAce: one of them sounds like *you*

OBenwhY: like me? huh?

PlanetSafeAce: no, like U
PlanetSafeAce: it looks like this: Ю

OBenwhY: okaaaaay?
OBenwhY: Ace I really really feel like I want to kick your butt to the moon right now, so—

PlanetSafeAce: here look: my way: SBЮBEN
PlanetSafeAce: the old way: SB1ØBEN
PlanetSafeAce: see how it looks almost exactly the same?
PlanetSafeAce: it was easy to create a new avatar name that—

OBenwhY: very divergent thinking Ace, congrats, no wonder Ms. J loves you

0BenwhY: but figuring out a way to fake Benicio's avatar doesn't explain WHY you did it

0BenwhY: WHY

0BenwhY: that's the real question

0BenwhY: does the Russian alphabet explain that?

PlanetSafeAce: i wanted you to notice . . .

PlanetSafeAce: the tiny difference in the name

PlanetSafeAce: see it, ask me about it

0BenwhY: so you wanted, what? You pretending to be my dead brother to be a GAME?

0BenwhY: or, worse . . . you wanted it to be some kind of TEST I had to pass?

0BenwhY: you realize that makes it extra mean and terrible, right?

0BenwhY: asking the kid with the dead brother

0BenwhY: AND dyslexia

0BenwhY: to find a RUSSIAN LETTER IN A FAKE AVATAR NAME?

I push away from the computer.
I can't even look at Ace.
I can't see anything.
Tears, snot, puffs of angry breath,
all of it streams out of me
as I finally
run
run
run
like I wanted to
in the first place.

RUNNING

I try to erase Ace
and everything
out
out
out
of my mind
as I
run
run
run
past every bus stop
past every house
past every thought
past every feeling,
until the only things
that survive inside me
are my pumping heart
and churning stomach
and all the sweat
and all the tears
still leaking out.

▫ ▫ ▫ ▫

I stop when my side hurts
too much
and my breath comes
too fast
and I can't figure out
if I'm going to barf
or pass out
or both.

Ben Y?

I look up
from where I lie
in a bed
of cool grass.

Why are you lying in Mr. Oppenheimer's yard?

Jordan squints and frowns,
kneeling down,
putting his face
closer to mine.
He has a puppy
on a leash
that also puts its face
close to mine.
And licks it.
A lot.

Are you feeling okay? You don't look like you're feeling okay?
Should I go get my mom? I think I'm going to go get my mom.

Jordan stands,
turns fast,
pulling the puppy away,
but my hand shoots out,
grabbing the back
of his shorts
and my words shoot out,
grabbing his attention back
to my face:

No.
Jordan.
It's okay.
Please don't.
I can't handle any moms right now.
Even a nice one like yours.
Did you get a new dog?
How did I not know?

I sit up,
shaking the grass
out of my hair
and then realizing

yet again
there is no hair
to shake.

Jordan sits next to me.
The puppy runs around us,
getting tangled in its leash.

This is a trial period of puppy testing to see if it's a good fit,
which means to see if we love each other, and I feel like the
answer is definitely yes because who couldn't love a puppy
and also who couldn't love me? Ha. Also I think the answer
is probably yes that I shouldn't listen to you and I should
listen to my guts telling me to get my mom.

I just . . .
I had a bad day
I'll be okay.

Except . . .
I don't know
if that's the truth,
and I can tell
Jordan can tell
I don't know
if that's the truth.

*I don't know if I should say this either, but you've had a lot of
bad days lately, Ben Y.*

I nod.

*And I probably definitely shouldn't say this, at least right now,
because I think Mo would say this is* inappropriate timing *but
even so, please don't be mad at me for being honest that I think
all of those bad days have made you kind of a bad friend lately.
I mean, hopefully not a permanently bad friend, but just so you
know. Lately. I mean, you didn't even know about Ben.*

Ben? Ben What Which Who?

Jordan picks up the puppy,
holds her up to my face
so we can boop noses.

Ben Hur, meet Ben Y. Ben Y, meet Ben Hur.

I shake Ben Hur's paw.
Ben Hur play-bites me
with her very supersharp
puppy teeth.

*I'm really sorry, Jordan.
I've just felt—
I don't even know how to explain it—*

but—

alone?

I guess?

Jordan shoves me,
pow
in the shoulder
hard and fast,
surprising me
as I topple over
into the grass
and Ben Hur
immediately
attacks my ears
and I scramble back up
to sit.

Who am I, then, you goof? Who is this human person sitting right here next to you right now? Who is the person right by you at school every day and on the bus and in Newspaper Typing Club and everywhere else you are? Maybe you feel alone because for some reason you've stopped seeing me even though I'm always there? Am I your invisible friend or some-thing? NO. I'm your real friend and when you have a real friend you are not alone, that is just basic easy math.

I can feel more tears
pooling up
behind my
already full
eyes.

Do I really make you feel invisible?

*Well, I mean, sometimes, yes, and I think Ben B and Javi get
kind of invisible to you, too, if I'm being honest and I definitely
am. And believe me, I understand that sometimes when you—
I mean anyone/everyone you not just YOU you—feels bad or
sad or mad . . . sometimes you WANT to be alone. I totally get
that and understand it and feel that way and yeah. But also,
you should just know that when you don't want to be alone, you
have a bunch of awesome and cool friends who are right there
in front of you and none of us are ever invisible at all.*

I nod.
I swipe at my eyes.

*Because if you can't ever see us trying to be your friend or
help you out, then one day maybe we could actually disappear,
you know? Because it feels really bad to feel invisible to the
person you thought could see you the best of any other person
in the world.*

Jordan untangles Ben Hur
from her knotted leash,
not looking at me.

I'm sorry.
I don't mean to whisper,
but I do.

Jordan looks up at me.
His big eyes are soft
and more familiar to look at
than my own.

*I know you are, Ben Y. But also I have bad days too and when
you don't see me, that makes ME feel alone. And it makes me
wonder why you want to be my friend if we can stand next to
each other and both feel alone.*

Jordan stands,
rubs his nose,
looks down the street,
looks back at me.
Ben Hur looks at me, too.

I'm still a crying,
sweaty
mess
in Mr. Oppenheimer's yard.

I'm going to get my mom for real now, okay? Unless you want to come with me? Instead of staying here and chatting with Mr. Oppenheimer? Hello, Mr. Oppenheimer! Your grass is very nice and soft. No, sir, Ben Hur did not poop in your nice soft grass. Ben Y didn't either. Haha. Okay, yes, sir. I'll tell my mom you said hi.

Jordan puts out his hand.
I grab it,
stagger to my
sore feet,
wobble on my
jelly knees,
and lean on his shoulder
as we walk
together,
with Ben Hur
nipping at our heels.

HOME

Jordan's mom drops me off
and does not
come to the door
like she said she would
because I beg her
please please please
not to.

(And also because
I'm pretty sure
she already called Mom
when I was in the bathroom
washing my face.)

Jordan waves,
holding Ben Hur
out the car window,
and making her wave, too.

I wave back,
and I may never stop
feeling like a big huge jerk

for making him
feel so bad
ever
at all.

▫ ▫ ▫ ▫

I walk in the house,
only just now realizing
I left my backpack . . .
somewhere.

Mom doesn't say anything
as she walks quickly to me,
gathers me in her arms
and hugs me tight
but not too tight.

Mom still says nothing.
She keeps hugging me
until I remember what it's like
to be hugged for real.
Not some quick one-arm thing.
Not some quick good-night thing.
A real hug.
Soft.
Solid.

Like Mom is holding me
and hugging me,
like she's transferring her strength to me,
one shared heartbeat
at a time.

She hugs me for so long,
I stop trying
to get her to stop.

I stop trying to
say anything at all.

I close my eyes.

I smell the shampoo she's used
since before I can remember.

I feel the tickle on my cheek
of her curly hair
that always comes loose
from her bun or braid or ponytail.

I feel my shoulders relax
as Mom's hug takes over,
holding me up for real,
holding me close right now,

blending our breathing,
like we used to do
when I was scared
or cold
or celebrating
or sad.

When did we stop doing this?
Why did we stop doing this?

I feel my feelings
rising up in me.

I feel Mom
hugging me tighter.

I feel Mom
wiping my tears.

I feel Mom
with me while I ride the waves.

I feel Mom
right here.

▫ ▫ ▫ ▫

You've been struggling.

Those are her first words to me
after we sit down at the table
with two spoons
and a crusty old gallon of ice cream.
I take a spoon.
Mom keeps talking.

I've been struggling.
Esme has been struggling.

I eat ice cream
and look at the table.
What am I supposed to say?
You're right?
Because yes.
And duh.
Yes and duh for a long, long time.

Your teacher called me today, mija.
The one you had in summer school?
She said it was an off-the-record,
not-official-school-business call.

She's worried about you, Benny.
She says you're withdrawing from your friends
and you're angry more than you're not.

She worries someone is bullying you.
She said she saw you run crying from the library.
She said you left your backpack.

Mom pauses,
lifts my chin so my eyes meet hers.
She smiles and says,
You were in the library?

I feel my blood heat up.
She's going to make a joke now?
She's going to laugh about me being so dumb now?

I'm so proud of you.

Wait.
What?

She said you've been working so hard,
on your typing,
on the school newspaper.
Benny! Why didn't you tell me about that?
But she also said you seem . . .
more sad than usual
and she's concerned.

I still don't know
what I'm supposed to
say.

So I fill my mouth
with spoonfuls
and spoonfuls
of old ice cream.

I let my crunching
of ancient ice crystals
do my talking
for me.

◦ ◦ ◦ ◦

Esme.

Always peeking,
Always peering.
A little sandpiper
darting here
scampering there,
just barely staying ahead
of wave after wave
crashing around her.

I see her duck out of the doorway,
run down the hall,
so she can pretend
she wasn't listening,
so I won't be mad at her.

Maybe she *is* struggling,
like Mom said.

Maybe Esme *isn't* a sandpiper.
Maybe she *isn't* staying ahead.
Maybe she's caught in the waves
just like the rest of us.

I never thought to ask her.

▫ ▫ ▫ ▫

Whatcha doing?

I lie on the floor
next to Esme's
bottom bunk.

She peeks over the edge at me,
then goes back to whatever it is
she does in here

every night
for hours
and hours.

Making stuff.

Her lower lip is chapped
because she sucks on it
when she concentrates.

She's been concentrating
a lot lately
I guess.

What kind of stuff?

Her sigh is long and deep,
like she's a grown-up
trapped in the body
of a teeny
sandpiper
eight-year-old.

Just stuff, okay??
Bracelets and things.

I push myself up on my elbows
so I can get a better look.

Tiny rubber bands
cover her bed,
separated into piles,
bright colors everywhere.

Esme holds up a bracelet.
Then another.
And another.

See?

Intricate color patterns
crisscross and weave,
surprising me
with how complex they are.

Kind of like
how Esme is surprising *me*
right now.

One for every outfit, huh?

She looks at me
like I am the dumbest person
who ever breathed.

I sell ten a day at school every day.
Two dollars each, Benny!
No one beats my price OR quality.
How do you think I got these?

She flings a foot into the air,
inches from my face.

Whoa.
Nice kicks, kiddo.

Don't say kicks, Benny.
No one says that.
How are you already so old?

Me??
How is *she* already so old?
She's yelling at ME
like I used to yell at Benicio.

I swallow hard
around the sudden lump
growing in my throat.

I guess I'm the old kid now.
I guess I should start
doing a better job

of seeing Esme
as the person she is
and not just
the little chirping bird
she is to me.

I stand up,
lean into her bunk,
kiss the top of her head.

I love you, Esme Esme bo-besme.

She doesn't look up
from the bracelet she's making
as she says,
You and Mom
are both
acting super weird today.

I can tell she's smiling, though.
And she laughs out loud
when I crack my head
on the bottom bunk
as I slide myself
up and away.

She chirps,
I love you, too, Benny,
as I leave her
to concentrate
on her empire-building.

□ □ □ □

I spin in Benicio's desk chair,
spinning
and spinning
and spinning
until . . .

Knock, knock.
Mom knocks on the doorframe
and walks in,
holding a stack
of clean laundry.
Benicio's pillow
is on top.

She sets it all down
on the foot of the bed
and then sits next to it.

Thought you might need this.
She fluffs the pillow.

So I can have something
to scream into?

I wish I could stuff those words
back in my mouth,
but thankfully,
Mom doesn't freak out.
She just nods
and shrugs
and says,

Maybe?
Or maybe to sleep on?
Or both?
You probably need a pillow
if this is going to be your room now.

She stands up,
hugs me tight,
and shuts the door
behind her.

BEFORE

OBenwhY: Helllllooooooooooo, nerd!

OBenwhY: Guess who has two thumbs and didn't fail her spelling test?

OBenwhY: Some girl who sits next to me. BUT! I *almost* didn't fail, so that counts, right?

SB1OBEN: har har. you're hilarious.

SB1OBEN: So! You wanna see something cool that has nothing to do with spelling tests?

SB1OBEN: You'll need some math, though.

OBenwhY: what is it what is it what is it what is it 😃

SB1OBEN: I've been tinkering with this potion for a long time.

SB1OBEN: Watch carefully. . . .

OBenwhY: but i can already see the world at my feet! ☺

SB1OBEN: Indeed you can. ☺ 🦗

SB1OBEN: check this out.

OBenwhY: whoa. I didn't know it was even possible to mix all that stuff together.

SB1OBEN: It's not supposed to be, but look.
SB1OBEN: you can dissolve fairy tears and it turns into this
SB1OBEN: but when you mix it with THIS
SB1OBEN: it turns back into that
SB1OBEN: and voila . . .

OBenwhY: pretty purple bubbles

SB1OBEN: Oh, it's so much more than that, grasshopper.
SB1OBEN: Here, take the potion and follow me.

OBenwhY: what are you doing?!!!
OBenwhY: put that theremin away! it's almost dusk!
OBenwhY: you're attracting so many ghosts with your bad music!
OBenwhY: I don't want to be slimed and melted!

SB1OBEN: Hang on and watch.

OBenwhY: Benicio!

OBenwhY: SO MANY GHOSTS!

OBenwhY: what does this have to do with your purple potion??

SB10BEN: Throw the potion at the ghosts, grasshopper! All of it! Now!

SB10BEN: . . .

SB10BEN: Niiiice. High-five. That was perfect.

OBenwhY: . . .

OBenwhY: whoa whoa whoa whoa whoa whoa

OBenwhY: what did I just do? did that potion melt the GHOSTS??

SB10BEN: _100_ can you imagine being able to build and play music all the time?

SB10BEN. Even at night with ghosts everywhere?

SB10BEN: can you imagine being able to defend yourself from your enemies?

SB10BEN: instead of just hiding from them until they prey on someone else?

OBenwhY: sounds like you're trying to make the impossible possible again

SB10BEN: ☺ Absolutely! That's what Sandbox is for!

SB10BEN: If people know this potion exists, and that there's a way they can defend themselves from ghost attac—

CHAT INFRACTION

SB10BEN: GAH

SB10BEN: if players know there's a way to beat the ghosts, it'll be HUGE, grasshopper

SB10BEN: think about it. if you know there's a potion you can use so that your avatar will never die, wouldn—

CHAT INFRACTION

OBenwhY: But can you even DO that? It changes one of the . . . what are they? Fun-what rules?

SB10BEN: Fundamental Rules of Sandbox. Yes. True. It changes a truth that ghosts don't die.

OBenwhY: well can you CHANGE that?

SB10BEN: it's MY game!

OBenwhY: i thought you said the money guys make you do stuff you hate all the time? like making stupid chat i—

CHAT INFRACTION

OBenwhY: ⬆ like making you invent THAT ⬆

SB10BEN: i know, i know.

SB10BEN: but what if this ghostkiller potion is my revenge?

SB10BEN: what if the money guys don't know about it and there's a leak?

OBenwhY: a leak?

SB10BEN: like, what if 😈 SOMEONE tests it out in public?

SB10BEN: just, you know, casually melts some ghosts?

SB10BEN: In front of a lot of players?

SB10BEN: On a public server?

SB10BEN: with the handy ghostkiller avatar I created?

SB10BEN: and what if people realize they don't have to hide in the dark anymore?

SB10BEN: they can play loud music

SB10BEN: and build all night

SB10BEN: and what if all that new knowledge goes viral?

OBenwhY: that's a lot of what-ifs.

OBenwhY: *what if* YOU get in trouble?

OBenwhY: when the money guys figure out you made this? and leaked it?

OBenwhY: you said nothing is anonomous anymuos GAH anonymous on the internet.

SB10BEN: 🙂 honestly, i don't really care. I want Sandbox to be fun again. for me.

SB10BEN: and not just work

SB10BEN: this seems like a good way to do that

SB10BEN: so . . . wanna be my partner in crime?

OBenwhY: UM DUH

SB10BEN: haha.

SB10BEN: ok, it's your turn to make the potion. Remember the ingredients? All the steps?

SB10BEN: you have to memorize it, ok? don't ever write it down. No one else can know.

SB10BEN: it's something players will have to figure out on their own

SB10BEN: they'll have to . . . wait for it . . . co-llab-o-rate, and list-en 🎸

OBenwhY: stop 💀 akjflhkgfdl i can hear you singing in my head. never do that again.

OBenwhY: And yes, I remember the ingredients. 👍

SB10BEN: 👐

SB10BEN: OK. Go harvest some fairy tears.

SB10BEN: We'll see how many tries it takes before you get it right.

SB10BEN: . . .

SB10BEN: Awwwwwwww shiitake mushrooms.

SB10BEN: Can you hang on a second?

SB10BEN: Or, actually, can you go gather up the ingredients while I do a quick work thing? I'll be right ba—

CHAT INFRACTION

SB10BEN HAS BEEN EJECTED FROM GAME

THIRTY MINUTE RESPAWN COUNTDOWN BEGINS NOW

NOW

OBenwhY: i hate to say it, but . . .

OBenwhY: i finally got your room

OBenwhY: please don't haunt me

OBenwhY: MOM gave it to me, so you can haunt her if you want

PlanetSafeAce: hello? oh good! you're here.

PlanetSafeAce: I wasn't sure you'd be here. After . . .

PlanetSafeAce: 😭 🏃

OBenwhY: of course I'm here. this is MY cabin.

OBenwhY: i really need to change the password now

PlanetSafeAce: I'm sorry I made you sad.

PlanetSafeAce: Even though I've been telling you I wasn't a ghost.

OBenwhY: yeah you told me and told me

OBenwhY: and I always knew you couldn't be him

OBenwhY: i'm not THAT dumb

OBenwhY: but still

OBenwhY: you kept using his avatar

OBenwhY: *why* did you do that?

PlanetSafeAce: I guess I didn't think you'd think I was interesting or want to talk to me

PlanetSafeAce: if I was *me* me and not me *him*

PlanetSafeAce: and then, you were kind of right earlier . . . I wanted you to figure me out.

PlanetSafeAce: I mean, not like a *game*, but just like you were really paying attention

PlanetSafeAce: bleh. that thought made more sense in my brain . . .

OBenwhY: how did you even get in the cabin in the first place?

PlanetSafeAce: you were in the library after school one day

PlanetSafeAce: I walked up behind you while you were on the computer

PlanetSafeAce: you looked really busy so I didn't say anything

PlanetSafeAce: and I saw you signing into the cabin

OBenwhY: THAT'S how you hacked in? You just saw me type the password? So low tech!

PlanetSafeAce: Yeah, I'm not a computer genius or anything.

PlanetSafeAce: you were, like, in the cabin chatting with yourself and that made me feel bad

PlanetSafeAce: like no one would play Sandbox with you or something.

OBenwhY: you low-tech hacked into my secret cabin because you felt SORRY for me???

PlanetSafeAce: No!

PlanetSafeAce: Well . . . kind of. Sorry.

PlanetSafeAce: but then I didn't think you liked me IRL

PlanetSafeAce: especially after I tried to take one for the team

PlanetSafeAce: that's why I freaked out and didn't want to use my own avatar

PlanetSafeAce: in case you got mad about the low-tech hacking, too

PlanetSafeAce: and also in case you didn't want to talk to *me* me.

PlanetSafeAce: anyway, i read a little over your shoulder

PlanetSafeAce: that's how I figured out you were (not) chatting with your brother

PlanetSafeAce: then i did a little research and figured out who your brother was

0BenwhY: OMG I WAS RIGHT YOU ARE TOTALLY A CREEPER. 😖

PlanetSafeAce: i know, i know. but i really, really wanted you to like me

PlanetSafeAce: and i'm always saying dumb things and acting like a weirdo IRL

PlanetSafeAce: and i wanted a way to sort of . . . *make* you want to talk to me

PlanetSafeAce: especially after I messed everything up by trying to SAVE YOU!

0BenwhY: save me?

PlanetSafeAce: Well . . . you saved me from the poncho thing! And I was trying to return the favor. . . .

PlanetSafeAce: . . . by saving you from the unauthorized Hart Times thing

0BenwhY: how did you even know it was me? who made the unauthorized Hart Times?

PlanetSafeAce: oh come on, how could I NOT know? You were smiling all day.

PlanetSafeAce: Like I'd never seen before

PlanetSafeAce: everyone else seemed so shocked about it, but you were just smiling and quiet

PlanetSafeAce: anyway, you seemed to hate me after that.

PlanetSafeAce: and i thought maybe i could get you to like me *before* you knew it was me

PlanetSafeAce: and i totally see now how that makes no sense

PlanetSafeAce: and how i'm pretty much the definition of an awful person

OBenwhY: is that all?

PlanetSafeAce: I'm not really sure what else you want me to say right now.

PlanetSafeAce: but hopefully you can accept my apology

OBenwhY: YOU USED MY DEAD BROTHER'S AVATAR TO TRICK ME INTO FEELING SAFE.

OBenwhY: omg, now that I really think about it . . . you took the only place I've EVER felt safe

OBenwhY: and you ruined it.

OBenwhY: AND you tried to take credit for my awesome unauthorized Hart Times

PlanetSafeAce: I WAS TRYING TO TAKE THE FALL FOR YOU, NOT CREDIT!!!!

PlanetSafeAce: sorry. continue.

OBenwhY: i haven't slept well in days. did you know that?

OBenwhY: you know what you *actually* accomplished?

OBenwhY: you managed to revive my Old Sad, create a New Sad, and mix the two up into a Now Sad.

OBenwhY: and for what?

OBenwhY: did your plan work?

OBenwhY: does it feel like we're friends now?

OBenwhY: does it feel like I think you're cool now?

OBenwhY: DOES IT?

PlanetSafeAce HAS EXITED GAME

SCHOOL

I don't know how I knew
but I knew

even though Jordan
wasn't on the bus,
he'd be waiting for me
in room 113
under the stairs
before school.

As soon as he sees me,
he crashes into me
like a much bigger Ben Hur,
and we hug it out
and neither one of us says anything
because we don't need to
and WHEW
I feel so much better
I might puke.

◻ ◻ ◻ ◻

I'm so glad—
and so lucky—
to feel so
NOT
alone.
Anymore.

□ □ □ □

Once we say bye,
I fly
to my locker
faster than ever
so I can try
really hard
this one time
to not be late
to class,
when
SLAM
the locker next to me
closes to reveal
Ace's face,
blocking my way
of escape.

I'm really really really sorry,
Ace says.

I sidestep,
start moving,
taking a different,
longer route
to class.

Ace jogs after me.
I pick up the pace.

I know you're sorry,
I finally say
to the air in front of me,
but I need
some Safe Space from Ace
for a little while,
okay?

Ace catches up,
walking fast
next to me now.

Deal.
Just please don't hate me, Ben Y.
You can be mad all you want.
But please, please don't hate me.

Ace's face is round,
open,
maybe even scared.

I can't have another Me hate me.

▫ ▫ ▫ ▫

The bell rings.
We are officially late to class.
Siiiigh.

I stop walking.
Ace stops walking.
I face Ace.
Ace faces me.

I kind of want to hate you,
but I don't hate you.
I'm MAD at you, but . . .
I could never hate you.
And mad is different than hate.
Plus, you're a Me.
And I'm a You.
And that means
this tiny group
of you and me
is the first We

of yous and mes
I've ever been
part of.

Ace smiles,
a lopsided
shy type of smile,
different
than the usual
24-carat-gold
sparkle smile
that comes with a wink
for free.

This is an under-the-mask smile,
a secret grin
from the kid
who cosplays
real life.

I bump Ace's shoulder.

So, yeah.
I don't hate you, Ace.
I could never hate you.
But I might need a minute
before we can be friends again.

The sparkle smile is back
as Ace exclaims
AGAIN??
SO WE WERE FRIENDS??

and we both laugh
and it's kind of loud
and I should've known
to never stop moving
in the halls
after the bell
because . . .

to borrow a favorite quote from Jordan:

[fart noise].

▫ ▫ ▫ ▫

AHEM.

The throat-clearing
is behind us.

Ace and I turn around slowly,
like every person
in every horror movie

before they get eaten
by a giant slime blob
or hacked up by a chainsaw.

It's even worse
than a giant slime blob
or an out-of-control chainsaw though:

It's Mr. Mann,
slapping his pad of detention slips
whack whack whack
slowly
against his palm.

Well, WELL.
Nice to see you AGAIN,
MX. Ybarra.
ACE.
Would you two like to BLAST OFF with me?
To . . . my OFFICE?

Ace shrugs and says,
No?

Rhetorical question, ACE.

Mr. Mann smiles big and bright.

Fire up your ENGINES, you two.
And set a course for . . .
my OFFICE.

◻ ◻ ◻ ◻

He said my office *twice*
and ruined his whole bit.

Ace's fresh-mint whisper
tickles my ear,
and I have to bite my cheek
not to laugh.

MR. MANN'S OFFICE

*We need to talk about
a certain . . .
UNAUTHORIZED
and ill-INTENTIONED
anonymous FLYER
that has been the TALK
of the SCHOOL.*

He crosses his arms,
looks down his nose,
at both of us.

*You KNOW
bullying is in FACT
a vicious ACT
that can happen
to ADULTS
as well as
STUDENTS.
And ZERO-TOLERANCE
means
ZERO-TOLERANCE.*

PERIOD.

His lips squinch
into the exact shape
of a cat butt
(just like on the flyer!!!)
before he gives us
whiplash
by smiling
big and bright
and saying:

But FIRST!
Might as well DRESS CODE you BOTH while you're HERE!
HAVE a seat.

Mr. Mann cheerfully grabs a pen,
gazing at the detention slips
like they're reflections of himself,
then he looks at me
up and down
in a way
that would get anyone my age
punched directly
in the face.

Stand UP.

I frown.

But you just said to—
My cheeks burn
as I stand.

Hands DOWN.
Fingers STRAIGHT.

He makes a
tsk tsk noise
and shakes his head.

Short shorts, AGAIN?

I mean . . .
they're just shorts?
My legs are long.
I'm tall.
It's Florida.
It's hot all the time forever.
I'm never going to wear jeans.

I don't say any of that, though.
I stay quiet.

I realize YOU think
your clothes CANNOT
literally HURT anyone,
MX. Ybarra,
but they ARE
LITERALLY
against district POLICY,
so I guess that means
WEARING them
DOES literally
hurt YOU.
HMMM?

I take the detention slip.
I don't say anything.

Now Mr. Mann looks Ace
up and down
and down and up
and his lip curls in a way
that I bet he doesn't even notice

because it's just a thing
his face does
all the time
when he sees anyone
like us.

I just don't know where to start!

His mouth opens
like he knows exactly
where to start,
but he doesn't get a chance
to start anything
because his office door
slams open
with a bang.

Before my head swings
even halfway around,
I hear Ms. J.

THERE you both are!
I TOLD you not to forget these,
but you were so intent
on running that errand for me,
you didn't hear me.

I might be a terrible reader,
but there's one thing I *can* read,
and that's Ms. J's face.
She's looking down at us both
and her eyebrows say,
GET UP AND GO.

I grab Ace's hand,
grab the two hall passes
from Ms. J's hand,
and together
we GET UP AND GO.

▫ ▫ ▫ ▫

Because we are the dumbest kids
in the history
of dumb kids,
we don't actually leave
the front office.
We pretend we're looking . . .
for something . . .
very important . . .
that Ms. J needs . . .
in the office . . .

and while we look for nothing,
we try our very very best
to hear everything
Ms. J and Mr. Mann
are saying.

□ □ □ □

Turns out,
we don't need
to try to hear anything,
because Ms. J and Mr. Mann
are talking really loudly.

□ □ □ □

When Ms. J shouts,

Well, I have zero tolerance for your whole attitude!
and then
Well, I think YOU should be suspended!
and then
What has HAPPENED to you, Malcolm?
and then
No, I think YOU have gone to the Dark Side!
and then
GET READY FOR A FORMAL HARASSMENT
COMPLAINT!

Ace and I decide
we should definitely
blast right out
of the front office
and definitely
set a course
leading us directly
to the safety
of the library.

THE LIBRARY

We run in,
shut the door behind us,
walk past the Planet Safe Space poster,
where someone has helpfully added
a drawing of a big bald head
just ahead of where my rocket is facing,
which I guess is supposed to be
MY own special planet
and har-har hilarious.
Not.

Ace takes the marker,
writes ACE on a rocket,
rips it off,
sticks it back on,
pointing the same direction as mine,
toward Planet Giant Head.

That's better.
Ace's hand goes up:
High-five!

High-five,
I say,
with a smidge of a smile.

□ □ □ □

Ms. J bursts into the library,
eyes flashing,
mouth set in a line.
She walks past us,
past the Planet Safe Space wall,
stops,
backs up,
looks at the Planet Giant Head graffiti,
at Ace's rocket,
at mine,
takes a step back,
then hurls herself at the wall,
tearing the poster off
in giant ripping chunks.

When she's done,
Ms. J faces us,
out of breath,
steaming mad.

□ □ □ □

So neither of you goes to class anymore?
Is that it?
Divergence is one thing,
but don't be divergent delinquents.

Ms. J's face softens.
Sorry.
No one is a delinquent.
I'm . . . angry right now.
About a lot of things.
I shouldn't take it out on you.
Even if you should be in class.

She pauses.
Is she waiting for something?

GO TO CLASS!
she yells at us.
Shoo! Get out of here!
I'll see you later at Newspaper Typing Club!

□ □ □ □

We walk fast
past the piles
and shreds
and pieces

of ripped rockets
and torn paper planets
and I hope Ms. J
has someone
checking in on *her*.

She might need
a teacher time-out
or some forest-bathing,
or something.

NEWSPAPER TYPING CLUB

*Uh, Ms. J, Ben Y told us you ripped down that whole giant
poster like you were some kind of angry wild animal who
hates posters and no offense but are teachers even allowed to
get mad and rip stuff off of walls like that? Do teachers have
consequences? You might get some consequences.*

Jordan seems genuinely worried.

Ms. J rubs her hand
straight down her face
like a mime
changing from a smile
to a frown
only her face stays
in a grouchy wrinkle.

*I appreciate your concern, Jordan,
but at this point,
I've lost track
of all the consequences
everyone at this school
including me
should face.*

She takes a deep breath.
Jordan breathes deep with her.
I don't even know
if he knows
he's doing it.

So.
How are your articles going?
Did anyone remember the deadline?
Which is today?

Ben B shuffles his feet,
Javier looks at the ceiling,
Jordan's *uh-oh* face
shows all his teeth.
I don't know *what* my face does,
and Ace says,
Here you go,
handing over at least three pages,
in a clear plastic folder.

When we all stare at Ace,
and no one says anything,
Ace's cheeks turn pink.
What?
We had a deadline.
Who ignores a deadline?!

Ms. J finds her voice first.
Well, thank you, *Ace.*
What a surprise and delight.

The rest of you . . .
twenty minutes.
Final drafts.
On my desk.

Twenty minutes?
Final drafts?
We glance at each other,
wondering who will save us now,
when the lights in the library blink off
then back on
then off
then on.

Mr. Mann is standing in the doorway.
He has campus police with him.

Shiitake mushrooms,
Ms. J breathes.
THIS is what it's come to?

▫ ▫ ▫ ▫

Everything in my guts
liquifies,
rising in a giant wave
of sloshing . . .
shiitake mushrooms.

Are the police here
for me?
For Ace?
For us?
Because of our clothes?
Because of the *Unauthorized Hart Times*?
Because we are literally against district policy?

Mr. Mann
and the police
advance
into the library
as Ace
takes big steps
backward,
and my feet
are frozen,
trapped
in this one spot.

▫ ▫ ▫ ▫

Mr. Mann

breezes past us, though;

the campus police

breeze past, too,

and

and

and

what in the *world*?

HART MIDDLE SCHOOL MAIN HALLWAY

It's just a suspension!
she yells over her shoulder,
her caftan whipping and billowing
like a flag just before a storm.

With pay!
She throws a thumbs-up at us
and a big smile,
even though
there's a campus police officer
on either side of her
escorting her
down the hall.

Don't worry about me!
She flings her head
over her other shoulder
as campus police hurry her
to the door.

She's outside now,
the electronic doors closing slowly
while she yells one more thing:

Obviously Newspaper Typing Club is canceled today!
We'll reschedule the deadline!

Javier, Jordan, Ben B, Ace, and I
stand in the main hallway
watching the doors lock tight
as our mouths hang open wide.

Out on the sidewalk
in front of the bus loop,
Ms. J says something
none of us can hear,
and Mr. Mann's
arms fly around
like he's being attacked
by killer bees.

▫ ▫ ▫ ▫

We all watch everything
through the big glass doors,
like we're all Jordans
and it's the season finale
of *Fierce Across America.*

Out of nowhere,
Ace turns
and bolts down the hall,
out of sight.

Jordan shakes his head,
sighing like a teacher
or a mom.

See. I told you Ace isn't part of the team. I could tell from
the very beginning. Because I could tell Ace was trying to steal
you away from me and be your new best friend and I didn't like
that at all and I mean, I guess it was nice that Ace tried to help
you not get in trouble, Ben Y, and if I think about THAT, then I
think maybe Ace is probably nicer than I thought, but mostly—
Oh.

Ace is back,
breathless,
Ms. J's purse in hand.

Figured she might need
her car keys,
you know?

Ace runs to the big glass doors,
holds up the purse,
shakes it back and forth,
smiles,
then mimes driving.

A campus police lady nods,
comes inside,
takes the purse,
says,
Thank you.

Ms. J gives Ace a thumbs-up
as she slings her purse
over her shoulder.

Ace does this thing in response,
a quick touch,
hand to chin,
then hand forward
then back down again.

Ms. J's eyebrows go up,
surprised,
as she smiles
and returns the
hand-chin response.

□ □ □ □

As Mr. Mann turns,
ready to come back inside,
none of us need to say anything

to know one thing:
We're not sticking around
to hear what HE has to say.

Ben B, Jordan, Javier,
Ace, me,
we run fast,
laughing,
sliding around corners,
racing to the stairwell,
and out the emergency door
that we all know
(except Ace,
who pre-winces)
has a broken alarm.

The air is hot,
thick with storms
boiling in the sky
as we run run run.

But even in the heat,
even with thunder rumbling
and lightning flashing in the distance,
it feels so good
to break free
from school,

from Mr. Mann,
from the hallways
from everything.

I hope Ms. J is right
and she's not in big trouble.

I hope maybe
she has a chance
to feel free
(at least for a minute)
while she also
escapes
Mr. Mann
and school.

▫ ▫ ▫ ▫

I could run forever,
with my friends by my side,
and I wonder
if this is how Benicio felt
when he packed his car,
and left for California
with Paul and Juanita
and a Sandbox dream.

We're all still running
and it starts to rain
and those big splats,
those splashing drops,
that cold water
making me gasp
as it drips
off my nose . . .
it makes me laugh
and laugh
and laugh
until I'm so out of breath
my laughs turn to
wheezing gasps
just letting it
allllllllllll
out.

Come on!
Ace motions
and we all follow,
climbing on the 315,
not knowing exactly
where we're going,
even though
we somehow
do know

(without anyone
saying a word)
that it doesn't matter . . .
not right now,
because the most important thing
is that we know
wherever we find ourselves,
we'll all be there . . .
together.

Jordan squeezes my shoulder
as I take a big deep breath
that turns into a big wide smile,
and I fall into a seat,
head pressed
against
the steamy window
feeling free
free
free
as everything
behind me,
behind us,
shrinks,
and the 315
picks up speed.

< NEWSPAPER TYPING CLUB CHAT >

ACE'S HOUSE

BenBee: but do you think she'll find it?

OBenwhY: for the millionth time, yes!!

JORDANJMAGEDDON!!!!: but why would she even go to the sandbox library if we aren't in Newspaper Typing Club?

OBenwhY: because she knows we're worried about her, silly. She's going to look for us.

jajajavier:): do you think she plays sandbox at home? without us?

BenBee: of course she does! who wouldn't?

OBenwhY: well, if she logs onto the Newspaper Typing Club server, she'll see my note.
OBenwhY: i spelled it into the grass. she can't miss it.

JORDANJMAGEDDON!!!!: these cookies are super yummy, Ace.
JORDANJMAGEDDON!!!!: how do I say thank you, again? touch my chin and then—

BenBee: you know we aren't in Typing Club, Jordan. You can actually talk instead of only chatting.

JORDANJMAGEDDON!!!!: I KNOW.

JORDANJMAGEDDON!!!!: well, I kind of forgot. but whatever. your grandma is AWESOME, Ace.

JORDANJMAGEDDON!!!!: your house is awesome, too. it feels very comfortable and squishy.

JJ11347 ENTERS GAME

OBenwhY: She's here!! Yay! See? I knew she'd find it! Are you ok ms j???

BenBee: Ms. J! Are you ok??? What happened?

jajajavier:): What happened?

PlanetSafeAce: What's going on?

JORDANJMAGEDDON!!!!: Are you getting fired? Please nooooooooooooooooooooooooooooooooo! You get suspended more than we do! 💀 akjflhkgfdl

CHAT INFRACTION

JJ11347: Calm down, calm down, everyone.

JJ11347: Thank you for worrying about me, but I am absolutely fine.

JJ11347: Not only am I fine, but I'm feeling very zen
right now.
JJ11347: I can't really talk about specifics, but my
job is safe.
JJ11347: It was quite a jaunt to get here, by the way.
This is a lovely safe space, but not easy to find.

OBenwhY: My brother made this cabin a long time ago.
It's not easy to find because it was supposed to be a
secret place where secrets are safe.
OBenwhY: I thought it might be nice to finally share it
with other people though
OBenwhY: kind of like a Sandbox safe space?

JJ11347: It's so comforting, yet energetic.
JJ11347: I really love the varying designs and colors.
JJ11347: It's fabulous work.

jajajavier:): check out IIIIS fabulous work!

JJ11347: Do we really classify blowing up a chicken as
fabulous?

jajajavier:): better?

JJ11347: 😄 Yes, everything is better with a confetti
cannon.

OBenwhY: and everything is better with you here, Ms. J

JORDANJMAGEDDON!!!!: Teacher's pet!!!!!! 🐶 🐱 🐸

BenBee: anyone see some marble? we should make a statue of Ms. J

PlanetSafeAce: the queen of taking one for the team! 🖤

JORDANJMAGEDDON!!!!: that reminds me . . . i'm sorry i said that thing, Ace, about not being part of our team. I was jeal—

CHAT INFRACTION

JORDANJMAGEDDON!!!!: and that was mean of me. Sorry. You ARE part of the team, and there is definitely enough Ben Y for ever—

CHAT INFRACTION
JORDANJMAGEDDON!!!! HAS BEEN EJECTED FROM GAME
THIRTY MINUTE RESPAWN COUNTDOWN BEGINS NOW

OBenwhY: no marble, Ben B, but i do have a test potion that will turn Ms. J into a statue.

BenBee: 😒

JJ11347: Ha ha. Hilarious.

JJ11347: Thank you for inviting me here, and I hate to chat and run, but

JJ11347:

JJ11347: I'll see you all *next* Monday.

JJ11347: Stay out of trouble!

OBenwhY: YOU stay out of trouble!

JJ11347: No promises. 😊

JJ11347 HAS EXITED GAME

Ben Ybarra

Newspaper Typing Club

AUTHORIZED Hart Times

First Draft

ADMIN SPOTLIGHT: A VICE PRINCIPAL'S JOB IS ONE OF THE MOST IMPORTANT JOBS

by Mx. Ben Ybarra

deputy editor

I like your alliteration but you can cut it.

Once upon a time, a possibly pretty smart kid said, "A middle school vice principal's job is one of the most important jobs in a middle school. Why? Because the VP creates harmony in the halls."

Ha Ha. Cut.

Who was this smart kid? Surprise! It was not me. Bigger

cut

SP:

surprise! It was Malclom Mann, the former deputy editor of the *Hart Times* (1987–1988). Yes. THAT Malclom (Mr.) Mann. THE Malclom Mann, current vice principal in the current halls of Hart Middle School. He used to be in eighth grade, RIGHT HERE. In the EAXCT PLACE where you are reading this today.

SP.

So, what does creating harmony mean, exactly? It does] Ha :-)
not mean helping students sing on their way to class.]
~~Well, it could mean that, but not in this case:~~ In this case] yes!
it means helping students feel comfortable and safe while good!
they're at school. ~~And~~ according to (Malclom) Mann (circa
1987–1988) this is the VICE PRINCIPAL'S JOB. Hmmm.

In his very fascinating article "Student Rights Are Human
Rights" (Malclom) Mann explains that students should be
treated like actual human beings, not dumb kids or crimi-
administration
nals or bad weirdos. He says "Teachers and ~~admin~~ and
staff should help make the halls feel safe for everyone.
Every student is equal and deserves equal respect."
choose one or the other
That is a [very good and smart point] (Malclom) Mann,
we know
~~former deputy editor of the *Hart Times* (1987–1988)!~~ this
SP: by now
If every student feels respect, (than) every student will
feel protected. ~~And~~ feeling protected means feeling safe.
~~And~~ if it is the vice principal's job to keep the school safe,
SP:
then boom, job done. [Harmony (acheivement) unlocked.]
Could be cut but I like it!
Thank you, (Malclom) Mann, ~~former deputy editor of the~~
~~Hart Times (1987–1988)~~ for ~~all of~~ your smart thoughts

about student rights and vice principals. ~~I guess there is~~

~~No Place For Your Face other than Hart Middle School~~ cut

~~since you are still here in the hallways every day. Kind of~~

~~like a ghost haunting a castle.~~ I hope you can learn how

to create the harmony in the halls (you're) younger self

thought everyone deserved. I hope you can figure out how

to help EVERYONE feel safe and protected. Maybe once

you remember how everyone, no matter what they look

like, or the clothes they wear, or the pronouns they use,

deserves equal human being treatment, then the ghost of

your younger deputy editor self can finally be really proud

of the Mann you have become.

I don't know if Malclom Mann ever heard this in the 1980s

(or ever), but:

Oh, Ben Y. Lovely.

I believe in you. You can do it. Make the hallways safe again.

♡

High-five!

Usually I would say cut the
High-five, but just this once,
you may leave it.